The Surgeon and the Climbing Boy

Mary Briggs

The Surgeon and the Climbing Boy

Olympia Publishers
London

www.olympiapublishers.com
OLYMPIA PAPERBACK EDITION

Copyright © Mary Briggs 2015

The right of Mary Briggs to be identified as author of
this work has been asserted in accordance with sections 77 and 78 of the Copyright,
Designs and Patents Act 1988.

All Rights Reserved
No reproduction, copy or transmission of this publication
may be made without written permission.
No paragraph of this publication may be reproduced,
copied or transmitted save with the written permission of the publisher,
or in accordance with the provisions
of the Copyright Act 1956 (as amended).

Any person who commits any unauthorised act in relation to
this publication may be liable to criminal
prosecution and civil claims for damage.

A CIP catalogue record for this title is
available from the British Library.

ISBN: 978-1-84897-514-9

(Olympia Publishers is part of Ashwell Publishing Ltd)

This is a work of fiction.
Names, characters, places and incidents originate from the writer's imagination.
Any resemblance to actual persons, living or dead, is purely coincidental.

First Published in 2015

Olympia Publishers
60 Cannon Street
London
EC4N 6NP

Printed in Great Britain

Mark Thomas Briggs
1985-2001

To Tim and Connie Hopson
(For their one-way friendship!)

Contents

Characters 11
Introduction 13
   'Wee Boys' 13
Chapter 1
   Jack Gets a Live-In Job. 15
Chapter 2
   The Surgeon 18
Chapter 3
   Jack at Work 21
Chapter 4
   Jack's Early Life 32
Chapter 5
   Mr Potts Meets Jack 38
Chapter 6
   Jack Meets Mr Potts 44
Chapter 7
   Sarah 55
Chapter 8
   Julia's Convalescence 57
Chapter 9
   Jack Gains a Family 65
Chapter 10
   The Final Part of Jack's Life 70
Chapter 11
   Looking Back to Julia's Wedding 79

Chapter 12
　　The Final Hours of Jack 87
Chapter 13
　　Jack's Mother Is a Mother 93
Chapter 14
　　Isobel 99
Chapter 15
　　Julia Thinks What to Do 106
Chapter 16
　　The Grave 110
Chapter 17
　　Juliet Returns to the Parsonage. 115
Chapter 18
　　Good News and Bad 120
Chapter 19
　　Albert's Reaction 127
Chapter 20
　　Julia Thinking and Alone 132
Chapter 21
　　Julia Meets Mr Potts 137
Chapter 22
　　Jack and Sarah - Consequences 149
Chapter 23
　　Jack And His Parents 158

Characters

<u>Julia</u> Sutcliffe   her mother and father, two sisters, her husband <u>**Albert,**</u> her <u>**Aunt Lisa,**</u> two sons, one of whom is Jack (future pregnancy daughter).

<u>Sarah</u>: Maid and chimney sweep, has a sister <u>**Rose**</u> **'wet nurse'** who has a daughter, <u>**Elizabeth,**</u> Julia's friend, <u>**Isobel,**</u> Master and Mistress **'**<u>**Soot**</u>**'**

The pastors, the WEAVER family, '<u>**Mrs Mary Weaver**</u>**',** two daughters, <u>**Ruth and Emma**</u>   their old maid, their pretty maid The Surgeon   Mr Potts, <u>**Jack Potts**</u> is the eldest son

Introduction

'Wee Boys'

Whoever thought of putting 'wee boys' up chimneys is unknown, but it grew as a practice in the eighteenth century, especially in London.

The 'soot trade', the dodgers, the dealers and the master sweepers, night men and apprentices, and the boys themselves, who had to climb up to clear the crevices and dark places in the chimneys, which became ever more elaborate.

The boys were often orphans and therefore had no one to oversee their welfare. They were usually unpaid and often treated with cruelty, but some 'Master Soots' were better than others. Some attempted to introduce education as well as chimney sweeping. If they did receive money from the customers, they could usually keep it. They usually 'lived in' with the Master Sweep. The apothecaries, the doctors of their time, often commented on their paleness.

Sir Percival Potts, a surgeon at this time, wrote of their plight, thinking the lack of cleanliness led to the disease; 'cancer of the scrotum'. Legislation did gradually improve their situation by the 1840's. Dr Potts was the first to identify an occupational hazard – soot impregnating the skin. The scientific name is 'Polynuclear Aromatic hydrocarbon'.

The sweep boys often only washed properly once a week. The sores and scratching would have made it worse. It was probable that they were given beer in many houses which would have eased pain but not have helped their unhealthy conditions.

Chapter 1

Jack Gets a Live-In Job

Jack was employed by the Master Sweep in the village because he was small, thin and poor. He could therefore climb up, or be pushed up, the smallest of chimneys, but he had the advantage of 'living in', as he thought of it, which was better than living to get by on the streets, and it became obvious that Elizabeth was no longer willing to keep him. He would miss his friends, but hoped to see them after church on a Sunday, on his day off.

He would have food, not a lot – he soon discovered – but he tried to be cheerful; perhaps he would be a master sweep one day and employ boys like himself. No one mentioned any pay but as he began working he found some customers would give him coins – the Master said he would look after these.

Jack was poorly dressed, though he did have two sets of clothes; one for the first week, the other for the next. He slept in his clothes and the soot dust because he was only really able to wash his face and hands during the week. He had a better wash early on Sundays in the yard, before church. The sweep wife would give him a clean set for church.

With no family, Jack was completely dependent on the Master so had to make the best of it. After about a year, he did begin to notice a red spot at the top of his legs during the quick outside wash with the bucket. He dried himself with some rags and often dressed himself still a little wet and cold. He liked to make sure the sore part was covered as it often got increasingly inflamed – he could not have known the repeated soreness would lead to skin changes.

Jack was living at the beginning of the Industrial Revolution when Britain would become the workshop of the World. He, of course, was at the very bottom of the division of labour but he was just relieved to have work and bed and board. He concentrated at trying to get better at the work, a little less afraid of the dark and the sheer loneliness of the cold when he had to climb. He put it to the back of his mind that he knew some boys had fallen to their deaths from high chimneys. As an orphan he lacked the kinship ties of family that would have made him feel protected. He knew, in his young way, that he was being exploited but at least he was inside, out of the weather at night and with a place to sleep.

He slept on a pile of old sacks, which in winter he soon learnt to edge nearer the fire, the range, partly because there was more light. He was rather afraid of the shadows as they leapt up the walls of the kitchen.

He was up early with the maid and she would try and give him a little of yesterday's milk. He thought he would like her, and did, and after the milk he went outside to see the sun come up and feed the chickens and check Jessie's water and say hello. Jessie was his friend, a rather elderly, black mare that drew the cart. The maid, Sarah, would meanwhile be lighting the fires and heating the water. When Sarah came back down, Jack was trying to get warm again by the fire – it was a chilly October.

She went across to work on the bread dough. He tried to be useful – she was always asking him about his birthday and his religion but he was not sure.

He knew, from talking to the other boys, that he was nearly at the age he'd be a man and his friends teased him when his voice got deeper. He wanted to stay friends with Sarah but often felt a little shy of her now. She was not the prettiest girl in the village but she was tall and took care to dress her hair very prettily and treated him like a young brother.

The Master was referred to by everyone as a Soot Merchant. Jack sometimes met other boys in the trade, from the local big town, and they would talk of how not to get too many coughs and fevers. They would laugh about how they got a bit 'silly' when they got the ale, but it did relieve the great thirst they got because of the dust.

Jack had soon noticed his patches of dry skin and his reddened eyes. He did eventually tell Sarah that he had some skin sores. He felt shy to do so, but it was getting worse. She suggested that he stole a little honey to put on the sore areas, to protect them with some clean rags to stop it chafing. She now tried to leave the honeypot out of the locked larder. He knew if he had told anyone else they would have told him off for being rather dirty. If he got the chance, he went to splash about in the river especially in the summer – his skin then looked better – on his Sundays, but this was autumn now and it was already difficult to stay dry as he had to stay out all day.

He had begun to notice that the skin had ulcerated and pain began to be a new problem, especially if he knocked himself.

Chapter 2

The Surgeon

Percival Potts would become famous as a surgeon with a fracture of the foot named after him to this day.

He was a theatrical character and when he fractured his foot he insisted he was carried on a door to the hospital because his carriage would have caused more injury, becoming famous in the history of medicine as being the first doctor to immobilise a fracture. He and his wife and children were living in a large house next to the parsonage at this time, in a village about five miles from a manufacturing town. Dr Potts had become something of a manufacturing pioneer and occupational health doctor identifying the diseases of the manufacturing process.

He had noticed that less attention was paid to the workers than the work they accomplished.

He was very Christian in his outlook, referring to 'the work of a creator – all benevolent'. He would see the chimney boys when they were at their cleanest; at church after their weekly wash and change of clothes. Potts had noticed that there were early deaths from manufacturing. He had noted that the so called climbing boys worked in confined spaces with clouds of dust and gas and wet vapour. He also noticed they had many changes of temperature and had few clothes with which to adjust to the changing weather and working conditions. He also felt angered that these boys were given beer as this probably exasperated the occurrence of accidents but he understood their great thirst.

Sometimes Potts would see the village sweep and the boy beside it or occasionally riding on the back of the cart, and felt glad the boy was getting some fresh air but would notice the apparent lack of a coat. He wrote in his books, 'for what a practice is health broken and lives destroyed.

He would later become very famous for seeking the connection between the boys climbing the chimney and an abrasiveness of their environment and a lack of proper washing facilities. Boys such as Jack. Potts knew could do little to remedy the discomforts caused by their occupation. Potts would later become the first doctor to identify an industrial disease with it exposure and association between scrotal cancer and the boys' exposure to soot.

Potts would often go and chat to the parson of his favourite subjects of what the manufacturing workers in the local town died of and at what age. The parson, a devout Christian, was as interested as he in the bad working conditions and living conditions he now often saw in his flock, especially in the town. The soot industry was a growing and powerful one. His doctor friend began to speak of his worry of the chimney sweeps' cancer as he got more convinced of a connection.

The parson knew the trade called these sores 'soot warts'. The soot warts were seen in young men after puberty and he knew were often mistaken for venereal disease. The doctor had explained to him the sores, if left untreated and unclean, could enlarge and become invasive to the nearby abdomen, causing great discomfort and pain.

Mr Potts told the parson that surgeons should remove the affected part.

The parson winced and held up his glass of wine to the fire to look through it, partly to distance himself from the surgeon's train of thought. He then drank the lot, needing a refill.

His doctor friend continued; the young men would then often be well for a few months but came back with a new occurrence and be much weakened.

The parson quickly drank all the refill.

After a little quiet in the study the two men would think instead of more cheerful subjects exchanging news of their children and arranging a musical get-together around the piano at the parsonage the next Sunday evening. They both felt some guilt that their children had only music entertainment to practise rather than having to work for a living while so young.

Chapter 3

Jack at Work

Jack was relieved to see that he thought he had been to this house before as he walked towards it, behind the cart and Master Soot. He was trying to remember the number of chimneys as well as the main chimney in the biggest room because that is where he would probably have to be of exclusive use and it would be dark, dusty and perhaps very cold or even a little bit hot if they had a fire recently. Master Soot was not an unkind man, but he lost his temper if sometimes things took longer than they should, 'time was money' he would mutter. Sometimes he would even rather push at Jack's body which would make the tops of his legs hurt even more; occasionally he would tell him to completely 'strip off' in order to get right into the space. This could be very embarrassing, especially if the housekeeper stayed anywhere in the room and he'd tense making the place feel very sore and sometimes bleed – which annoyed the sweep even more. He wore a sort of sling of rags around him to stop this showing. Jack was trying to remember if he'd managed to steal a little honey this morning, as Sarah had told him to do, to put some right on top of the sore.

Jack tried to dismiss his fears by looking up at the sky before he went into the house and patting Jessie's rump while the Master spoke to the maid.

They were to go to the back of the house, which was a parsonage. Jack could hear a brook nearby as they went round to the back. They had been very busy all day and the nights were drawing in, it being October, and a lot of the customers preferred, or even insisted, that the sweep arrived in daylight which made for less hours for the Master to make his money.

Jack had wanted to get a drink from the brook but did not want to upset anybody. There had been nothing at all to drink at the last house. He did have a chance to pick a couple of apples – late apples – as they passed round to the back, without being seen. They were old and a bit dry but Jessie would be delighted with hers – Jack gave her one and the Master looked over hearing the horse munch and scowled, "It'll be me who loses the work if you are caught scrimping and taken to court." Jack shivered, if only Jessie could eat quietly – the boys were always telling him about how the local thieves and robbers were punished in public in the court. Water and drink would be good but he knew how ale helped him cope better, though it made him a bit sleepy, especially if the afternoon was drawing on, and the Master would cuff him because he was also weary.

He edged up to see if he could stroke Jessie's nose while they waited – it was too risky to slip her a second apple on this well-kept drive. He hid the forbidden fruit at the back of the cart. Master Soot started shouting for him to hurry up and bring the brushes. The Master usually took the long brushes into the house but in his hurry, because it was beginning to be dusk, he had gone in with the small brushes. Jack was forced to get the two big ones off the cart and had to drag them making him limp a little with the pain. The sore was itching as well, which made him want to drag the brushes and scratch at the same time. He felt embarrassed. He had a last look at Jessie and at the lovely red sunset coming over the hill behind her adding a bright orange shadow to her mane and ears. He felt better but the day had been so long and he was so tired now. The housemaids were tut-tutting sympathetically because he was so small and carrying two big brushes. Then he realised somebody was carefully helping him with the other end. He looked round to see the housekeeper gingerly lifting the end with a duster cloth and an "ugh" and a sympathetic smile. And he knew this must be one of the lovely houses – he always remembered these.

They were directed into a kitchen which was lovely and warm and welcoming, making him want to dawdle and gaze around for a jug of water or ale. The housekeeper said, "You are limping, lad."

They went through the house, holding the brushes together to the front room. They went in and it was so late in the day the housekeeper said they were just to do the main sitting room chimney tonight and if possible call again tomorrow which was a Saturday. Everything was prepared with dust sheets. The two housemaids were smiling at him, having heard about his limp. There was an older one, who did the tut-tutting and sang snatches of songs at him and a younger one, so pretty he could not really look at her. He did not know it, but the handsome blush made him look so much better the young maid blushed too.

Jack had followed the Sweep in wincing a little the large brushes had pressed on his breeches and therefore onto his sores. His thoughts were a muddle – what if sweep just wanted him barely dressed? He was already embarrassed, this pretty lass had seen him very dirty in his Friday clothes. The Master was already scowling his frustration at them when the housekeeper couldn't see, "Less money, laddie, and an earlier start tomorrow." The pre-Christmas season was his busiest.

Jack heard from the conversation that this was a parson's house. The housekeeper kept smiling round at him – she was a lot friendlier than what he was used to. Usually servants got a little tetchy if they thought dust was setting or spreading.

"The boy will need a drink," the Master surprisingly said. He hoped for one himself but also wanted this large chimney clearance to go well. Jack was so relieved, as well as astonished that the Master was being thoughtful. He did not know that the Master knew the parson was well acquainted with the doctor apothecary who lived next door and the sweepers had all heard the rumour that Mr Potts was trying to get the practice of climbing boys stopped.

The older maid brought Jack a lovely cup of stream water – he would have preferred ale as it seemed to relax him for the task but then he remembered sometimes he got a bit giggly if he drank it quickly and hated the thought of embarrassing himself in front of the pretty maid.

At least the chimney was cold – a little too cold as it was dusk. Sometimes the cold made his whole body shiver and shake and ache but at least, he thought, this was to be the last chimney today and, "It has been a ten hour day," the Master said to the housekeeper thinking they might give him an ale.

Master Sweep began by laying his own dust sheets and the maids brought screens to seal them off completely. Jack wondered if the maids were pointing at him out of concern; he was trying not to limp and draw attention to himself. He loved to look at these screens which were often old but with beautiful painted birds and flowers.

Master Sweep was beginning to rush now taking the medium brush and making a lot of soot fall. Jack was beginning to hope his physical entrance into the upper large space would not be needed.

Next the Master used the big brush; Jack was having some difficulty standing still now due to his nerves and tiredness. He was not allowed to start sweeping up yet so he quietly slipped down onto one knee lifting his breeches to ease the pain.

"Come up in the left side and we will be done." Master Sweep was more of a worried man than a specifically unkind one – he quickly helped Jack get his feet astride the side of the large chimney and placing the smallest brush in his hand, and with an 'up' began to push him up into the space. As usual Jack quickly shut his eyes, opening them just as little slits when he had to. He pushed up with the small brush making him breathless and having to spit out with his mouth and breathe through his nose as well as keeping his face a bit downward. He was so relieved not to hear the word climb; this was what he dreaded when the Master wanted him to go up even higher balancing with bare feet on the side of the chimney. One dreadful time the chimney was so hot he had burned his heel and his elbows because he had lost his balance and had had to steady himself sideways.

This present, smaller, easier route went on so long he did not know for how much longer he would have to keep rubbing his nose although it was always a little sore but as each new dust cloud lodged against the wall and fell, it did help him breathe more easily. If he had had ale it would have prevented this present sense of panic he was feeling.

Then, thankfully, the Master began to ease him down and out of the chimney – he quietly sank onto one knee again to stop the trembling that made him feel he might fall over.

Opening his eyes again, having hopefully squeezed away the dust, he realised a pair of ladies boots were right in front of him and he lifted his eyes to see the housekeeper gazing down at him.

"Thought the boy was just an assistant apprentice, we do not approve of boys being used for clearance." She sounded angry –

staring down at Jack, who quickly got up. He was rather confused; this had never happened before and he was startled.

The Master looked at her, lost for words – never had anyone made such a comment and this was a woman speaking to him like that. There was a brief shocked silence with Jack hurriedly getting up although he could not stop trembling – had he heard the lady right?

The lady turned and went off back behind the screens; thank goodness the Master had not asked him to remove his clothes. The soot was yet to be collected. He quickly helped the Master, they were both coughing because there was so much dust and it all rose again. They seemed to finish quite quickly, not speaking at all – and then Jack saw when the screens were opened a maid offering him a small cup of ale and a large one of water – but still where was the Master?

Jack gulped the ale in relief as well as half the water and, without thinking why, handed it to the Master to drink. The housekeeper was back – staring at Jack.

"The lad's pale and he was limping. How old is he?" she asked.

"Twelve," the Master guessed quickly – he had as little real idea as Jack himself.

"If he is ill," she went on, "We have a very nice neighbour who is an apothecary and surgeon, he has been telling the pastor about chimney sweep boys and the illnesses that they get, and he said that he would rather that the practice was discontinued."

Master Sweep grunted a reply, touching his cap politely, he wanted his dinner, "We'll be back at eight tomorrow to do the rest of the chimneys," he said to change the subject.

Quite soon they had completed the tidying up and had replaced all the tools back in the cart to the relief of Jessie, who knew she was now on her way home. Rather unusually, the two maids helped them – smiling at Jack – but grimacing as they got sooty. Jack managed to slip the apple into Jessie's ready mouth from the back of the cart and, to quicken their departure, the Master said Jack could ride on the back beside the brushes rather than walk back to the gate and the lane. Jack did so, hoping Jessie did not mind his extra weight at the end of his day. A maid just then dashed out with some fruit cake wrapped in a cloth for Jack and a carrot for Jessie, she said Jack was to give it to him later – Jack blushed it was the pretty maid with the big eyes and the flaxen hair.

The Master from the front of the cart just said 'giddup' to Jessie. If he had another climbing boy he'd make sure they were not as sweet looking as this one – mind you, the old ladies also loved him so it probably helped trade.

They got back in the dark – Jessie knew the lanes and there was some moonlight.

The Master was so tired now, he absent-mindedly let Jack deal with Jessie after she was uncoupled. Jack led her into the stool afterwards.

She was an old horse and preferred Jack, who made a fuss of her. Most of her food supply was under lock and key. He was limping again but checked her water and kissed her nose.

The Master's wife was a little less bad tempered than she could sometimes be, putting a bowl of milk in front of him and some bread, but no butter, and then some stew.

After going to the toilet outside Jack went over to his sleeping place. He would have a warm up by the fire later, probably with Sarah, after the couple had gone through to their sitting room. Sarah must have had her supper already. He had a small treasure trove of things such as a picture book that someone had given him – it had some writing in it but he was unable to read. He wished he could wash himself properly tonight to ease the pain but also to look better for the pretty maid tomorrow morning, he realised with a blush, but at least he could have a small wash this evening. Perhaps Sarah would have found some ointment as she said she would – she had said she'd ask her sister, Rose, who she saw on Sundays so this next Sunday might bring something to make it better. Jack had been embarrassed with Sarah about it but she said a lot of the boys who did this work got soot warts. He had felt rather worried about what the housekeeper had said – would he have work and a place to live if he was not allowed to climb in the bigger chimneys? Sarah would be down soon and they could talk about it. She was allowed a bedtime drink and they would have a whispered conversation near the fire. She could read a little and sometimes they would look at the Bible together because she knew a lot by heart so the words would say themselves partly. She hoped to teach Jack a little so that when he was a proper sweeper he could do his books.

Afterwards he would sleep often, dreaming of riding Jessie flat out to rescue Sarah from bandits. Tonight he dreamt of the maid with the beautiful eyes, who had been told of his bravery.

The boys, who spent the day with him come rain or come shine, often asked him about Sarah. They were intrigued that they were just the two servants together. They had often asked him about Elizabeth. They knew Elizabeth had not been his mother – some had heard rumours that she had sold Jack to the sweeper to get some money to pay to live behind a shop in the nearby manufacturing town where she now worked.

Jack would be upset but pretended not to be. He had less and less memories of her – she had always seemed so sad and worried – someone had said she was a young widow without children.

Jack did not tell the boys what he knew of Sarah; that she just had the one relative – a sister, Rose – her husband worked on a farm so they had a cottage. The boys teased him that Sarah would be his sweetheart. He would get embarrassed. Sarah was the sister he wished he had – when he was older he wanted to be a Master Sweep and pay for himself and Sarah to run a little farm or they could both work in one of the new big houses on the edge of the town – the boys all wanted to work there – they were grand houses with many servants and more food than you could eat.

Too soon it was early morning – breakfast would be gruel and bread. Then Jack and the Master Soot were off again while it was still dark, with Jessie walking sleepily as the sun began to light the road. Jack felt himself walking a little better today. The Master had got Jessie ready himself for speed, wanting to get out earlier for the extra visit, as he had lost money yesterday. He had told the wife of the strange incident of the housekeeper and her comments – they both worried, as other sweeps did, about the doctor with his new ideas.

It was not far to the parsonage and the bright sun picked out all the colour of the trees – Jack was trying to count how many chimneys the parsonage probably had and wondered if he would get more of that cake from the pretty maid – he'd scrubbed at his hands and face. He had slept well because he had eaten so well last night. He had had no hunger pains last night.

He did not think he had to climb at the parsonage knowing the housekeeper did not like it. He felt a bit puzzled himself about it all and told Sarah – would he not have a job? He had heard from the other boys about apprenticeships and he and Sarah had wondered if he could get one – then he would know the trade, but Master Sweep had never mentioned teaching him the 'job'. But he did not want to change too much – he loved the horse and Sarah looked after him. He heard from other boys that under servants at the big new houses had too much food and their own beds. They often slept at the top of the house altogether with landing views of the river and learnt to cook, perhaps one day in the future, if he could not be a proper sweep, he could be an overfed servant somewhere.

The housekeeper and the maids were all smiling at Jack again, making him blush, and said they were pleased he was not limping. Hiding his blushes by looking after Jessie, he heard the housekeeper tell the sweep that the doctor next door would be interested in seeing Jack tomorrow after church at the parsonage. She said he usually came over to take a glass with the parson after the service and suggested that Jack could walk the short distance from the church on his own – she seemed to emphasise that looking at Jack then adding to the sweep, "Because then Jack would be nice and clean after his change of clothes for church."

Without waiting for his answer she turned round to Jack and said the doctor was very nice and there was no need to be at all worried. She added that he had been a famous surgeon in London and was interested in young people and that Jack had had a limp and a quick look would not hurt.

She emphasised the words about Jack being a youngster whilst looking round at the sweep, who laughed uncertainly. He wanted to say this would not be necessary but Jack had been limping and there was no mention of money, and a replacement younger boy might now be better and it would also give Jack an occupation for a change for Sunday – the parson might feed him.

The sweep insisted Jack and Sarah stay out all day after church on Sundays, whatever the weather – Sarah had often wished her sister would let Jack come over sometimes but she would not and Jack liked to see his friends even if he often got soaked in the fields by the river – Sarah contented herself by finding a treat for him to bring back.

Yes, the sweep said, if they got on with all the chimneys. Jack felt more energetic – scanning the corridors for the pretty maid between chimneys.

Unusually, the sweep and Jack were invited to sit down in the kitchen and have some refreshments. Jack and Master Sweep had never sat down and eaten together before and Jack was so relieved to be having a rest in a lovely, warm room, so much so that he flopped in a chair by the fire before being asked. There was no ale but there was lovely warm milk a piece of bread and a cake. Mr Sweep even seemed to relax a little as he edgily sat gazing into the fire. He had decided not to worry for a bit. This was seasonal work – cleaning all the chimneys ready for Christmas – you had to maximise the day light.

Jack quietly hid some cake for Jessie, not that Sweep would wait while she ate it, if she ate it.

With a friendly wave back at them, Jack followed the cart back to the lane thinking that that was the best house they visited and wished it could be more often than twice a year. He need not have saved Jessie some cake – he was given some more wrapped in a cloth with an apple each for himself and horse.

Chapter 4

Jack's Early Life

Jack, of course, does not remember his earlier life. Jack had been born illegitimately to the youngest daughter of a mine owner in a market town fifty miles away. In fact they had the biggest house in the town and were rather an exclusive family, due to the father's rapid accumulation of wealth. The mother was very strict and was determined that her three daughters would marry well, into the gentry. She, herself, had been born into some poverty, making her even more ambitious for her daughters; she had been exceptionally pretty and had mixed with the rising young men of the area and had married very well.

Julia, her youngest, was always her favourite, partly because they were so alike, with lots of curls, an easy manner and pretty ways.

The mother often wondered if her youngest would be the first to marry. She would later often blame herself for what happened, but there were so few signs of impending trouble. She had often noticed that Julia would chat to a nice, but shy, young man called Mathew who often came to stay with his relation in the town, as the two young people were such good friends anything of a more romantic nature seemed improbable and put the mother off her guard. They were the good-looking favourites of their social group.

Once things had got out of hand, the mother could not work out how or why, but the first worrying sign was that Julia changed in character. She became strangely quiet and hesitant and sometimes tearful, the governess was the first to voice her concern.

Julia's mother did not, in fact, care much for the governess, thinking she was inappropriately bossy with the girls but she was anxious to remain on good terms with her husband who had appointed the governess himself and so she bowed to his wishes. He thought the governess a little too strict but maintained this was good for his girls, and they were excelling in their French speaking, literature, needlework and music.

He also failed to see a change in Julia; partly because knowing she was his wife's favourite he rather left things to his wife as regards her last born. *The youngest is often the closest to the mother*, he thought.

It was a family practice for the girls to spend more than two hours a day being schooled in the morning and then often they would have reading and music in the afternoon and then the evenings were spent sewing.

The father was frequently not at home so that the mother tended to be the one that sent the invitations to the young people. She loved to see the young people happy and finding their way out to the world of men.

Julia, of course, knew that things had gone too far with Mathew and in her fear about her changing health and mood told herself it would be all right. But as the months passed and she was sick so often clandestinely, the governess eventually told her mother of her concerns. Yet even then the mother did not think of Mathew because he had stopped visiting his relatives locally and therefore no longer came.

As soon as the mother realised what the real problem was, the (four) women closed ranks and even without really discussing it they went into an overdrive of solution to avoid scandal and protection – five months had gone by – Julia was 'blooming' to look at but very quiet. It was quickly arranged that Julia was to go to the coast to her Aunt Lisa's, to support her aunt and for her own health as she had a cough. "She will be back in the spring for the new season." Julia's father was never told and never really asked questions, although he thought six months was too long. Julia had had a cough for quite a while the family told people, and a change of air, particularly sea air, was ideal. There had recently been a lot of consumption in London, she said, and you can't be too careful of the young. So the mother had carefully contrived a solution that the father never did know about and the governess was dispatched to an even better position up north with an excellent reference, a large painting gift and the tactful understanding of censure.

The careworn looks of the wife the husband put down to increasing age, the 'change' and that she was missing her favourite. He missed his youngest, particularly that Christmas.

So Jack was born at the seaside to a frightened fifteen-year-old mother and taken away immediately – Julia had had a home birth, prearranged at a local, trusted doctor's discretion.

Julia managed it all – the loss, the upheaval – well on the outside but inside her the scar never would heal. She was told it was a boy and was allowed to name him Jack.

The same doctor had discreetly arranged for Jack to be lodged with a wet nurse and her family. Janet was well known and trusted by the doctor – she had a daughter, Elizabeth, who was rather headstrong but also childless so the doctor thought the solution might unfold with Elizabeth. Jack had been born to great wealth but would now live much more moderately. Money followed the child for a few years for expenses and payments but these quietly slipped as

Julia's mother and Liza no longer had the means to continue the expense privately.

So later, when Janet the wet nurse said that a lovely permanent home had been found for Jack there was no one to ask questions. So in fact, when all payments had ceased, Jack had already moved with Elizabeth to a manufacturing town twenty miles away where Elizabeth hoped her feckless husband would settle down in employment – which never happened – so Jack was 'sold' with little sorrow to the village sweep. Elizabeth eased her conscience by assuming he was taken on as an apprentice. She did miss his angelic-looking curls and shy face – he had always been rather nervous of her husband who hadn't wanted the expense, especially as any payments had ceased.

The baby had not been registered and the wet nurse had a large family so Jack had just been passed hand to hand as another child.

Jack had been an affectionate but rather timid child.

He realised Elizabeth was not his mother. He was a very good-looking child and the sweep thought his naturally polite manner would please the customers. The competition for Master Sweeps was intensive so they had to think of extra attractive things to make their business grow. Large chimneys had become something of a status symbol for the wealthy – they were increasingly difficult to safely clean.

Mrs Soot had not been able to have children and had at first rather overindulged the timid boy and he was given his own room to sleep in because they could not yet afford a kitchen maid. He was the good-looking boy that fetched and carried for the sweep. He grew a little taller approaching puberty – he wished he had a mother and, as the Sweep's wife withdrew emotionally, he expressed his love with the horse and stray dogs until Sarah came to take on the role of sister.

There was never excess food and the Sweep's wife was not well – Jack did not really realise he did not have the basics – he looked forward all week to the Sundays with his friends whatever the weather.

He did miss having his own room when Sarah came and he had to make do with his cubby hole in the corner of the kitchen. But at least he was near to the animals and the range. In the summer, once finished for the day he was free to roam about letting himself in and out of the back. None of his Sunday friends lived close enough to see during the week – he became rather introspective. He always received quite a lot of attention from the lady customers who would make a fuss of the boy. If he was really needing company, he'd sit with, and perhaps rather annoy, the lone cow once he'd milked her. Sometimes they had a pig, getting fatter and fatter for slaughter, he hated that. He hoped to be out working when it happened. He was relieved not to be included in that side of the smallholding.

Jack did not understand the economic downturn that accompanied all the competition. He noticed there was less food and more ill temper; this increased the bond between himself and Sarah and their whispers and plans for a better future.

Mr Soot was rather an unemotional man who had been rather relieved not to have the expense of his own children. His main interest was in building the business to have a comfortable life. Mrs Soot felt her childlessness and withdrew into herself; she liked Jack for being quiet and little trouble. She had little knowledge of children thinking if you fed them a little they looked after themselves. She tended to feed her husband well as he was the breadwinner – but also insisted one needed a maid – *Sweeps' wives have maids,* she thought. She began to notice Jack was not so well, that he was coughing more and she guessed that he had trouble with his skin and that Sarah helped him – even stopped locking up the honey jar thinking that was the answer and left the pail by the door with clean rags. But Jack was so tired at the end of the day and outside the door now after dusk was too cold and she knew children got taller and thinner as they changed into manhood.

With growing her own vegetables and looking after a smallholding, the Soot's wife had become rather limited in her thinking. She did not join in much with wives of the village and attended church infrequently as she had such little family news to share and pray for.

She thought Jack must be twelve or thirteen, not remembering how many Christmases had passed; not that presents or celebrations occurred even then.

As Jack looked more unwell she had suggested to her husband that Jack go instead to work at one of the big houses with the other lads where he could live in – and they could get another younger boy but her husband said they would keep Jack for a couple more years as Jack was so polite and well-liked by the customers – he regarded him as an asset and helped the business to stay afloat no matter what Dr Potts might say.

The wife herself had misgivings about the boy's part in her husband's trade. She had seen the burns on his elbows and heels but she knew the poshest of the houses often asked for or even demanded a climbing boy's thoroughness. If Jack went to another job they would lose trade and earning power. Jack in fact did 'pay for himself' and was a big part of why they could get by financially, so he did deserve more and better food. Mrs Soot also thought brushes would get better and chimneys get smaller and more manageable without the use of boys.

The Sweep had little idea that Jack had become ill because of such work.

Chapter 5

Mr Potts Meets Jack

Mr Percival Potts – Sir Percival Potts, he had been knighted – was going in to see his friend, the village pastor, who lived next door. Today he wished he was not. His wife had told him there was an ill-looking climbing boy the pastor wished for him to see, knowing that he had been investigating why these poor soot merchant boys so often got sick and died so young.

Mr Potts usually enjoyed having a cup or glass of something with his friend but disturbing his Sunday afternoon was unwelcome.

The young man may indeed be sick and frail – the description may even be morbidly so, regretfully he nodded his assent to his wife. It was just after midday and soon they would sit down to Sunday lunch as a family. Their servants had attended church with them and were busy in its preparation, after which the servants had their own. The house of the well-known London surgeon was very well-organised.

Mr Potts loved the peace and quiet of his Sundays with his family, his children vying for his attention, later in the afternoon they might read or walk in the lovely garden together; and with the use of a Sunday rota the servants took it in turns to have a Sunday off to visit their families. This was a household very much based on Christian principles of work and rest. Mrs Potts ran a well-organised home for her increasingly famous surgeon and medical writer husband.

Fighting the wish for a pre-lunch read or conversation, Mr Potts told his wife he was walking next door to the parsonage to have something of a drink with his friend and see the boy.

The autumn was gathering its pace in its beauty, there was a little chill in the air and the trees were bright with colour. He wished really that the parish could have dealt with this – he tended to try to balance his home and work life.

The parson's wife, Mary, greeted him at the door with a half-smile – she immediately said this was the only one occasion and that it would not happen again. Mr Potts brushed aside her worries and went to have a glass and chat with his friend in his study.

The pastor was rather uncharacteristically unsmiling, Potts thought. The pastor began to explain that the village Master Sweep was efficient but he insisted that he needed his lad because chimneys were getting too big in the new houses and the pastor knew that their two wives had discussed the surgeon's worries about such work. Worries about the health of the climbing boys.

The women had realised that this young man was not the sweep's own boy, he had no children; but the lad had somehow become attached to a woman, they thought was called Elizabeth, in the nearby manufacturing town. This woman had probably been abandoned by her husband and could not afford to keep the orphan. Now of course where he was he did have 'bed and board', the pastor winced – this probably meant sackings and left over food – but the pastor continued – the boy did look noticeably unwell, was limping and the winter was coming.

Mr Potts had sat himself down, having helped himself to a glass of port. They were both feeling pensive –both aware that living in did not necessarily mean living well and as they had their glasses of wine they were both thinking of the many beer drinks given to quieten and give courage to the boys in their dark, dusty work. This also made them a little giddy and perhaps a little dangerously reckless. The pastor unnecessarily then reassured his friend that being Sunday the lad would be relatively clean for church in 'fresh' clothes. He emphasised the word fresh with a sad smile. *Makes you want a refill,* he was thinking but gazed at the fire for inspiration instead. There was a thoughtful pause.

At the morning service, Potts had glanced across at the parish servant boys, the local poor boys, wondering which it was he had heard he might be asked to see. They were clean in their Sunday best but many looked ragged and thin. They were usually very well-behaved – much better behaved than the well-off children he always noticed.

Mary, the pastor's wife, often gave them a drink of milk or apple juice and some bread and cheese or pie, he thought, but he guessed the real reason that the servant boys were better behaved may well be sheer exhaustion and long-term malnourishment.

Apparently this lad was coughing and at times seemed to be in some sort of pain and his nose was running and his eyes seemed scabbed. Master Sweep, when questioned by the housekeeper, had swept any worries aside, 'has a cold as appens' and the pastor continued, regretfully the lad had been put up to sweep one side of the chimney. The housekeeper blamed herself for this because she'd noticed the lad was limping and had thought he was just a helper or an apprentice. The housekeeper knew well there was increasing disapproval of climbing boys.

Mr Potts stood up and stretched to try to curb his Sunday sleepiness and gave his friend a quizzical smile and led the way back out of the study. They went through to the parlour together. This was a large bright room with a lit fire. Mr Potts went straight across the room to the fire ostensibly to warm his hands, in reality delaying the moment for the lad who he knew would be nervous. He had seen the lad out of the corner of his eye, he had seen so many of these ill gentlemen he could almost diagnose on the spot, with an eventual life expectancy with some accuracy.

Now he glanced over as he warmed his hands. The lad was sat on a sturdy chair but you could almost hear that he was trembling – he was predictably small for his age – post puberty at a glance, thin, pale, frightened and understandably overwhelmed.

The pastor, who had held back, now went over, "No need to be afraid, Jack, this is a very famous apothecary," he thought the word might be more familiar than doctor and less intimidating. "He will be able to help you, he'll sort out any skin problems that may be distressing you and see why you sometimes limp." Mr Potts quietly approached the lad whose eyes were huge in this thin face.

"Have you had your dinner yet?" the big man asked kindly. Jack nodded though he had missed the hand-out after the service, worried he might get late and his stomach had rumbled – the housekeeper intended to give him a proper Sunday dinner – the parson laughed a little and said he thought his wife had a meal for him before he went off to see his friends. He knew the practise of 'out all day whatever the weather' some of these employers had for their live-in workers.

The doctor pulled up a chair beside Jack, privately looking at the boy. He felt sure he already had a soot wart and his lungs were probably already affected and he may well be a terminal case because it would already be too late to remove the affected part – the boy would not survive such a procedure, Mr Potts speculated. He gently asked him if he had any sore places down below and if so, how long it had been sore for? The lad had no real idea of the time span of his problems – this was typical of such an unfortunate boy in these circumstances. Mr Potts knew such boys were too busy just trying to survive in their competitive trade. The lad coughed – going bright red, in embarrassment looking a little healthier momentarily because of it. Then his eyes ran, whether with tears, the effect of the cough or with fear they could not know but the pastor's wife Mary had come in behind them a very practical and kind woman – now moved forward to invite the lad to the kitchen for milk and apple cake. The boy followed the pastor's wife out with relief, limping a little though he did not know, but the doctor saw.

The pastor looked at his friend – knew he did not need to ask and they both went to sit at the fireside without speaking.

Eventually the pastor said, "I'll use my influence with the soot merchant." After a while added, "There might be some friends we can use to compensate him." He was already thinking of a post for the lad as a gardener's assistant at one of the well-kept houses – they were Christian people but would the lad be well enough? The parish did have some places at the workhouse in the town – young, poor, not well and without family, his thoughts would only run on that line.

Mr Potts still said very little, but eventually got up saying, "Let me know and I could come back and examine the boy – not today, he's had enough today." He knew he may well include this sad case in his ongoing study of cancer scroti— cancer of the scrotum."

He paused at the door – this needed to be said, "He may well not last too long," they were well out of earshot. Potts patted his friend's arm – doctors were used to these circumstances, pastors not necessarily, especially at the diagnosis stage.

"The sooner we can get rid of this climbing boy practice the better."

They both knew they'd settle back into their family routine of a good family Sunday lunch. These two families often got together later on a Sunday evening for some songs around the piano and poetry reading perhaps they both gave thanks for the robust health of their children in their thoughts as they quietly parted.

Chapter 6

Jack Meets Mr Potts

Back to Jack

Drawing some sacking over him, although it meant less under him – Jack was lying awake worrying about meeting the famous 'apothecary' the next day – which was a Sunday – he had only slept fitfully. He thought of dragging his bed sack heap nearer the fire thinking he would be awake anyway before anyone came in so he would not be in trouble with Mrs Soot for moving things about – but he was trembling and tried to get warmer where he was.

    The day ahead seemed dreadful, although it was his day off. The sackings could make his sore part worse if he was not careful to pull his breeches aside. He now heard them moving about above him so he got up and went over for a quick warm. He knew he had a rather chilly wash in the yard with a bucket ahead of him before breakfast. He knew the sting of the sore would be worse as he washed so he thought he would pour the water over himself. The sore seemed quite swollen more so than before, sometimes it bled a little. He had put some honey on it – Mrs Soot left the jar out – it seemed to be for his exclusive use now thanks to Sarah. Like the other boys, he would shout at and tease the local girls but he had a reverence for Sarah – she was different – like how he imagined a sister would be.

She came in first with a quick smile. He had told her that he had been asked to see a doctor about his limp after the service. Jack brought out Sarah's mothering instinct. At age seventeen she hoped to have children herself one day. She gave him her usual tap on the head. He still has his lovely curls.

Mrs Sweep was, as usual, a little bad-tempered. She would have preferred to lay in bed on a Sunday but she did look forward to having the house to themselves later. They would have a big dinner then some quiet. The girl and lad would be out all day.

What they did or ate, she didn't know and in truth did not care. She was not a bad woman and sometimes felt a little guilty and looked out a bit of cheese and an apple; but she felt rather anxious today about her husband and unpaid bills from the big new houses at the edge of town that they had been regularly servicing. Prompt payment helped them through the leaner winter months when chimneys were too busy and often too hot to be swept. She glanced at the boy as he came in – she felt a bit worried knowing he had a skin problem – the houses that did need them in December and January would be overheated she knew.

Barely speaking, she mixed up the gruel to cook on the fire and seeing again his thinness in the old clothes, she gave him a drink of yesterday's milk. The cow would be milked again soon anyway.

The boy shivered as he drank – the water was warming on the fire ready for his wash before church. In a spasm of kindness she said, "Here, lad, and warm up," pointing to the mat – the girl was busy elsewhere. "Take those things off and put them in a pile and I'll put the bucket out beside the door." She and Sarah both realised that he was now grown and became more embarrassed on Sundays wash day, so they left him to it.

The boy trembled by the door as he eased the dirty clothes off his sore place and then he washed as best he could – he was rather startled at how different in size his man parts down there were but he got on quickly. There was some throbbing pain because the clothes had got stuck with a little blood on the sore and so he carefully patted it with the cleaned rag but the rag was still rather stiff in the October chill.

He had moved the honey pot nearer him – his honey pot now – and it hurt as he applied it. He reached for the clean shirt and breeches hoping he was dry – he was hoping to quickly get back to the warm fire but felt a little giddy. He knew the gruel would come soon, which would be steaming hot. Mrs Soot's back was turned; Sarah was smiling at him, knowing he was nervous about the doctor, looking over at his honey pot questioningly. They had wondered if the doctor would tell them off about the use of honey.

He knew he would be out all day, so he had his jacket and cap and boots – quite soon he and Sarah left to walk up the lanes to the church. He did ask Sarah to wait while he just popped in to say hello to Jessie and a goodbye. He always enjoyed his Sunday walk with his 'sister' especially as today the weather was bright. They would be early so they dawdled a bit. Sarah knew he would not want to talk about the doctor again – he could tell her all about it later that night. They joined the others and sat in the park till the sexton let them go in. He liked to sit with Sarah but still let himself imagine what it would be like when he was 'walking out' with a girl – he knew some of the other lads about his age already said they did.

The church did seem a bit colder than the park to him today but he felt a bit sweaty sometimes and the sore throbbed at times. He had decided he would spend the afternoon in a sheltered spot beside the river rather than charge about with the other boys – chasing girls if he could – he might have a chance to have another wash.

He felt a little fearful knowing that he would have to walk alone to the pastor's house – he tried to catch Sarah's eye and give himself courage. The warden came to do a reading with them, and then the congregation began to come in. He loved this part of his Sunday, watching the pretty ladies in their beautiful highly fashionable clothes and their gentlemen in frock coats and high collars that seemed to make their faces redder as they sang hymns and gazed at their sweethearts.

It always lifted young Jack's heart when the church was quiet and he could imagine himself with a family or a sweetheart to look out for. He always prayed for his parents, believing them to be dead, they would be able to look down on him and see his loneliness.

The warden seemed to know that he was going over to the parson's house, he thought he would have to wait with the others but the warden rather friendly patted his shoulder and said, "You can come over now I think they have some cake for you."

'Cake.' Jack nearly fell over hearing of this unexpected kindness in his present high nervous state and went off, enjoying the beautiful walk through the gardens, it was so peaceful. He felt better and carefully made his way round to the back where he knew the kitchen was. He was rather hungry after the long service. And this must be the housekeeper – yes it was – he remembered the gentle smile. He was brought before the fire with cake, milk and various servants coming in and out and the children of the house – some coming to have a look at him and smile before they got some cake. They put his cap and coat to warm. He sat back – perhaps he was in heaven already and his mother would come in too. He sat in the warm, surreptitiously easing his breeches away from his sore place. They were always talking of hell's fire at church he thought as he nervously watched the flames in his shyness at being such a centre of attention.

Some while later, the housekeeper herself came and took him through to the parlour to wait. "You've nothing to worry about, Jack, the doctor will be in to see you in a minute, he's just interested in helping you boys who might have trouble with your skin because of all that soot." Jack was too overwhelmed to realise that this doctor might have something better for his sore than dabs of honey.

The parson came in to tell him the doctor was coming to his study and then he'd be in just to see if he could help. A little later a tall big man came in, glanced at his direction then walked across to warm himself at the fire. Then the doctor came to join Jack and the pastor pulling up his chair and a little sombrely explained about his dinner and later the man asked him about his skin and any sore patches that he may be able to help him with. Jack spluttered an embarrassing cough trying to concentrate on what the man said. The man did not want to examine him after all to Jack's great relief. And the pastor's wife was asking him back to the kitchen he thought. He left the two important men with some relief – he felt a bit sleepy and somehow not so afraid anymore –he really hoped he could find somewhere for a sleep before he went back to his own house later. Sunday supper at the Soot's was sometimes a bit better because it was the leftovers of the Master's own meal – meat, vegetables and sometimes sweet pudding. He was so comfortable back before the kitchen fire he had some trouble not to doze but the pastor and his wife returned, rather staring at him – making him blush again – he was a naturally shy person.

Then he could not believe his ears as they said the doctor had said he needed light work until he was completely grown up.

"Mother, here," the pastor pointed to his wife with a smile, "is going to find you a bed for tonight and we will all look for an easier job for you in the morning – in fact, Mary, take him up now and let him have a nice sleep and perhaps, a bit later, he and I will have a talk this evening."

Mrs Weaver led the nonplussed Jack upstairs with a maid following into a bedroom and offered him a chair – while the maid to his astonishment was busy lighting the fire. Trying not to be rude he looked around; there was a bed, a rug, a wardrobe, drawers and the chair he sat in. Did they mean this was all his for tonight? His room? The maid asked with a smile if he would like a bath later. He was a bit wary. He knew that rich people got into big metal containers wearing very little and called them baths. The lads would laugh about it – would they not see his sore, all these people were women. The maid coloured a little herself and said the pastor's two boys could help him if he wished.

These people seem to want to do what he wished. He was not sure whether to be afraid or excited in his confusion – would it get better more quickly then? Then he remembered that he had put honey on the sore – would they be angry? Meanwhile, Mrs Weaver was directing the maid to check the boys' cupboards for some warm clothes, "Robert's his size I think."

"These were clean today," he quickly said. "I'm sure we have lots of warmer clothes for this time of year – I think that is why you may be a little feverish – you have not got warm enough clothes on." She did not want him to feel rushed into anything – she had told the family to get on with their dinner, she would have hers later.

What she did not know was that her husband was already striding down the lane to Master Soot's cottage. He made himself walk a little slower, realising he must not arrive in this angry state. The interview he was to have would go better if he was calm. He patted the pocket where he had put the cash to ensure a smooth deal.

The couple were half asleep, having just finished their puddings but felt obliged to invite him in. Trying to be a little casual, the parson said, "Let's sit down," and promptly sat himself down at the table where they had left the remains of the meal for Sarah to eat with Jack before the clean-up.

They felt embarrassed, which was to his advantage. "Nothing to worry about but Jack had a vapour after church," they made a point of showing concern, "So my wife took him into our house."

"A nice, polite young man," he made a point of seeming complimentary, soothing the worry. "As Dr Potts lives next door," he paused here while they registered this; for the soot industry had got word of the surgeon and his worries about the climbing boys, "I asked him to visit. We have put him to bed after a nice bath," he could not resist adding, which probably was not true but he had caught sight of the sacking sleeping space.

The man and woman looked startled, staring across the table at one another – Master Soot then sort of jumped up, rattling his chair unable to know what to say.

There was a short silence.

"Is he better now?" queried the wife of Jack. "His supper is here, ready," she said, looking at the leftovers – Jack's supper?

"Oh hush, but the doctor does feel he must have lighter work I'm afraid – due to his small stature and the fevers."

Finally the soot merchant found his voice, "We can't work without him, what will I do tomorrow?"

Quickly the pastor said, "I've thought of that," he got the purse out, "the parish will compensate you – I think he will be working up at the monastery, so it will all tally."

The pastor felt strangely at sea – he had lived fifty years but had not had to think of what you would pay for an orphan so he was really rather generous with the parish's money.

The couple clearly wanted him gone, they were quietly pleased about the amount on the table – if Jack was ill he could not work – they had the best end of the bargain.

There was a terse polite thank you and shaking of hands over the 'sale', then the parson left. He was hungry as he walked back, wondering what was happening now at his home? And wondering about this new theology – the price of one of God's young men and his work, in sickness or in health – to the world?

Jack, meanwhile, had been shown a big, but still unfilled, tin bath and lots of fresh towels. Curious maids hovered, one even holding her nose – but Mrs Weaver took hold of the situation and said the young man could have a short soak and then a bit of a sleep only if he wanted to and showed Jack a soft night shirt.

Some tears of embarrassment came, so she sort of hugged him briefly thinking to get aprons and one of her sons and the older maid or her husband – where was he anyway? Then making everyone go and shutting the door, she spread the clean things out and helped him undress.

"I've got two big lads of my own," she laughed, turning her back to him.

With the clothes off, the smell of the sore was stronger – she recognized it as a smell of putrefying flesh, she had sometime smelt this before, on older people. *A cancer probably,* she thought. Nearly in tears now herself, she suggested he just put the night shirt on and lie on the bed for a while,

"Bath later," she said. She covered him with a sheet just for soft protection and a blanket, "We'll get some more milk."

While they waited for the maid to fetch it, he relaxed a little trusting her more now. Without asking, she drew back the covers discreetly to have a look at the enlarged sore place and then also saw the hollow chest, the scabbed face still a little wet with embarrassed tears.

"I can't get it better." He seemed to feel ashamed.

The maid came in with the milk and helped him to sit against the pillows to drink: this was an ill young man, how old was he really? How very sad to be so ill so young. The second maid was the older jolly one from the day they had cleaned the lounge chimney. After she had exchanged a look with the mistress she said, "So, what's your favourite song?" and sang to him to distract him. His fears were less because she had enchanted him. Nobody had ever sung for him before.

The parson arrived on the landing and his wife whispered to him, "Get Percival back if you can, I've never seen anything like it."

The two maids instinctively kept him covered up and amused him till they thought he would sleep. Later, once he had slept, the surgeon came back and just politely had a little look at his sores, 'cancer of the scrota', now so advanced the boy would or should never have to work again – for this was probably the final part of his life; would he see Christmas?

"Nice gentle bath if and when he wants, I'll send some ointment to apply to the sore and prescribe some tincture for him to take if there is pain." There seemed to be a general consensus that Jack would stay with them. It was all unplanned but none of the family thought for a moment of any other solution.

So, this last, sad, very short part of Jack's life began that Sunday afternoon at the parsonage.

The bath was embarrassing but soothing, the older maid showed all her skills now – as a nurse – he was soon back to bed, lovely and clean with the ointment applied. He would meet the parson's two sons later, they hoped their help might be less embarrassing and also thought they would hire a male attendant – Dr Potts would know.

A maid was allocated to sit with him.

He woke only for more milk, hoping for ale just because he was used to it to soothe him – he had never felt so comfortable in his life. He had fresh lint covering the sore. He only woke to use the bucket beside the bed. The only sound in the middle of that night at the parsonage was his coughing. Downstairs the parson and his wife could not settle to sleep, they felt they were rather now in, and almost part of, the gospel story – they wondered at their own comfortable life and Christian values, and realised some of the flock savagely flaunted and ignored the care of the young people for the sake of profit – the truth was there were uncared for children to trade with.

They knew that with this advanced disease he could not live long – there was little smell now, they had burnt those old clothes in the garden and tomorrow would tidy his curls and help him cut his nails, and planned to try to fatten him up a little so that he could be up and about again. Their own four children did not appear to resent all the attention being on Jack, their new lodger; perhaps the whole family could give him some sort of childhood – a shortened childhood spent quickly and fully. So without discussing it they both assumed he would stay there with them.

Mr Potts himself was more used to these situations but it tried and tested his faith in a benevolent creator as he thought to refer to God. The servants seemed eager to help.

Mr Potts did not say so, but realised this gave him the chance to observe the illness. He felt some guilt at knowing he would be taking such an opportunity but knew it would strengthen his resolve to get this trade to stop using youngsters to clear the big chimneys of the wealthy without resource to good food and washing facilities. He would now get even more evidence and use his position as a man of influence, to stop this abuse – all thanks to his friend, the parson, and their family.

Chapter 7

Sarah

When Sarah got back on the Sunday, she was feeling a bit anxious. Normally she would see Jack around the village as she made her way to her sisters or on the way back from Rose's cottage down the lanes to the Soot's house. But she had not seen him at all.

As she went in the back door at dusk she glanced over expecting to see Jack sitting waiting for some supper with her, she had not seen him at all after church.

The Mistress Soot was standing with hands on hips staring at her without speaking. She motioned to Sarah continuing to gaze at her without speaking. Sarah felt quite scared now, had something happened to Jack? Perhaps he had been silly, he had looked so pale this morning at church. Sarah was glad that he had found some honey at least. Sarah had heard about these sores that soot boys get. They can get infected and make the boys very ill she thought.

So Sarah and Mistress Soot now sat down in some silence; Soot's wife was gazing past her out through the grimy window at the darkening sky, Sarah was waiting, was Jack lost? "He's gone – he wasn't coming back."

'What?' Sarah gasped.

"The parson said he was ill at church and he will find him some lighter work at one of the gardens of the big houses." Soot's wife did not mention the coins handed over, in payment for the child.

Sarah found herself in tears, Jack was important to her she had long realised; she would go and see him but she was also suddenly relieved for him as well. Working in a garden might relieve his leg. But then she thought of the winter to come and that he would be working outside, he was so thin for such outside work.

But then, thinking quickly – she thought how the parson's family were friendly and kind and they had boys of their own. They might give him some warm clothes, a hat and coat and good boots?

"Did you see him having the vapours?" Soot's wife thought she would use the opportunity to find out what had really happened.

'Err, no, but he was pale and his leg was hurting I think when I went to see Rose.' Sarah was cautious now it was a bit controversial telling the Soot people that these boys got bad legs because of the rough, dirty work – she was a bit surprised when Mrs Soot then said, "I know," but Mrs Soot herself wished that she had not said that. The truth was she was also worried knowing of the rumours about soot boys getting ill; and her husband had told her that some houses refused to allow for the boys to be used which made the job, and planning for it, more difficult for them all especially with this fashion among the rich for larger and more complicated chimneys, and the growing competition for the work between the traders. She was worried about the money they always seemed to owe their suppliers. They never seemed to get on top of their debts and stay there.

She wished she was a lot richer as a soot merchant's wife, with prettily dressed children of her own and less grinding daily work. *You can dream* she thought to herself.

Chapter 8

Julia's Convalescence

As the nurse and baby left the room, Julia turned to the wall and wept; she could not think that the baby was being taken away – she had to think she was giving the baby away to someone who desperately needed a baby and would care for him and because she had no other choice.

Ashamed and afraid of feeling terribly alone her huge sobs left her so exhausted she slept.

She awoke to find some fruit juice beside her ready to drink, she knew she had to 'lie-in' for she thought for as much as ten days. She had no idea at all how she was going to do this – refusing the mirror the maid offered her to tidy herself up – eventually she did accept the warm water for a wash and then let the maid tidy her hair and began to feel a little better, if only that ache in her heart would leave her. She read books if and when she could and did some grieving. Her breasts felt tender and a little milk sometimes came out. The bed was beside the window so at least she could watch the countryside. No visitors came that day or the next except the servants and the doctor but she was so healthy she had no post-natal problems.

After some days Aunt Lisa did come, but she did not stay long – she was rather shocked to see the tear filled eyes and they were not to converse much. The baby was not mentioned at all; Julia might have been recovering from flu.

Aunt Lisa had children, two boys – older than Julia – who were told she was here for a rest and to help cure her 'cough'. They also had a young daughter who had no interest in Julia.

Julia tried to quickly fit into her Aunt's family as best she could. She liked her cousins John and Paul but they had been told she needed to rest so carried on busily with their hunting. Julia had never been for so many sea walks normally with her Aunt; she had never read so many books or painted so many pictures.

"You are to go home at the end of next week – which will be nearly the start of the new season," her Aunt said to her enthusiastically one day. She was to take two days for the journey and a Miss Baxter was to accompany her.

Julia's figure had changed and filled out making her look even more handsome. Miss Baxter proved to be prim and appropriately friendly but they found few subjects in common to discuss so they were quiet on the journey. Julia felt a little nervous when they stopped for the night, as had been arranged for them to stop at an inn half way. She had not recently mixed with many people other than the family and now all the people, especially the men, seemed to stare at her, so she asked to have her meals brought to her. She knew she would have to conquer this social phobia that now was apparent to her; she was also trying to think how she would deal with her return to the family.

Once she had arrived home, their carriage clattering up to the front door she should have felt joy to be home but everyone was a little tense, noting how uncharacteristically quiet she had become. Her 'cough' was obviously cured. There was a very embarrassing moment when her relieved father rushed in to see his youngest, asking if she had found some nice husband material by the sea? Wasn't there a naval college near there? How had Christmas been – all balls and parties?

She was so relieved to finally get back to her own room to be alone but was immediately sad because all her collections of baubles and bright things – especially the dolls – her lovely china dolls now meant so little. She was already aware that her relationship with her mother had changed. Her mother's eyes were full of sadness, although her lips smiled and laughed with relief to have her favourite home. Her mother was also desperate to put all this sadness behind them – but she could not – Jack was of course her first grandchild.

Neither, of course, could the new 'mother' – Julia put it all behind her – she was changed for ever.

Her sisters, she knew, were still prospecting good marriages – as they thought she should still go on to do. But she felt she could not. She thought she never would be able to – but nothing of this was ever discussed by the family. It was as though the six months 'convalescence' had cured Julia's cough, now she was expected to throw her beautiful self into the new social spring season.

Julia therefore had no one to tell that she felt like a fallen woman, and also how little she had understood that phrase before. She herself lived comfortably, and had a supportive if rather unserious family of women to talk to. The question of blame was never addressed either, but the change was in her mind and her soul with a seriousness about life that she had never expressed before. She was living in a county at the centre of financial and social progress. Women such as her were meant to party and meet and marry suitable partners and begin lives of family and prosperity not lives of disappointed children. In her heart though, she told no one she had swapped one predicament for another. She carried on meeting her friends socially telling them she felt so much 'better', that her health was strengthened – she danced and sang – but the enthusiasm was no longer there; so the more perceptive among her friends noticed how changed she was in her outlook. Men, entranced by her good looks, showed an interest but she was cold and could not really respond to them.

Not one person of her acquaintance ever mentioned Mathew – he seemed to have completely 'disappeared'. Mathew had known and had told her his father's business was in trouble, which was why he had behaved so out of character with Julia at that fateful time. He had been told that he must leave his relatives who lived near Julia to travel to his grandparents because his own family home had been sold due to his father's business failure. He had really loved Julia and hoped to propose to her but filled with shame as events spiralled downwards he had broken down telling her his plans. That summer night they had gone off alone to talk and somehow in the summerhouse sheltering from rain they had made love, an experience she could never forget or really regret. They knew themselves to be in love – later they re-joined the party having not really been missed –but very soon after a coach was announced for Mathew – he was whisked away by a relative.

He soon thought of sending her the love letter of what he was feeling but the family news was so grave he had nothing now to offer a wealthy young woman – even if he knew he loved her. For many years, he was to be found working as a clerk at a merchant's in London, still hoping to reverse his future and perhaps approach Julia, whom he had not forgotten. But he knew such a beautiful woman would probably be married by now. He never knew of baby Jack.

Julia was seen to smile less, but her figure was fatter and more curvy and buxom and she still had the most admirers of the three sisters – despite her sometimes solemn face.

Her two older sisters were soon to be betrothed and married and she was the bridesmaid, still refusing marriage proposals herself. Her mother was amazed and concerned – she had assumed her youngest would do what other good-looking young women would do – marry and thereby fit right back into society, as nubile and marriageable as before because nobody knew of the real tragic change.

But the sad fact of daily life for Julia was Jack. She had barely been able to glimpse him. The birth had not been problematic, it was his complete absence and the complete absence of news of him that seemed to unhinge her battle to get over it all as well as she had hoped to do. Each day she thought of her missing child.

Her father, meanwhile, had decided to move his family to the next town which was rapidly expanding as the industrialists bought up the large houses at the town's edges. Julia's mother was pleased with the move. Her two married daughters already lived there and she hoped the move and new acquaintances and a new social life would invigorate her youngest. The mother felt Julia needed the busy distractions of her own home and family then the lost child would fade from memory.

The child, her first grandchild, would be growing fast now because Julia was already twenty-five now and the boy – her sister had given her this one bit of information that it was a boy – would be secure with his new family.

Julia and her parents, the three of them, moved into a vast house in the new town taking most of their servants with them. Julia was nearly getting to the end of her so called 'marriageable' time of life in these days; her mother became increasingly worried about her. To her parents' relief she now did meet an older man who was a widower, though without children; Julia increasingly longed for a child – a replacement child – though few, of course, knew and the widower Mr Albert Sutcliffe longed for a family. She sensed that he had a beautiful house and some years had passed since his bereavement. What attracted Julia was that he was something of an intellectual – they would have conversations together about society and even women's positions in society. It had been very hard for Julia, although she told no one, the life that she had lived as a single woman without any real intimacy and Julia felt deeply attracted to this man in a way that surprised her. She realised she was very much in love and desperately wanted to go to bed with him.

One evening, as they were dancing, she found herself overwhelmed with these lovely feelings she thought might never come back to her again – wanting to hold onto his hand in the dance, unable to look up at him – but it was the same for him as he gently drew her aside and almost mumbled a betrothal in a fatherly way thinking she would reject him. She lifted her eyes and said 'yes' and both a little overwhelmed they left the window and went back into the dance, their eyes locked. When the dance finished he escorted her back to her chair and she saw him go over and quietly ask her father if they could have a talk – her mother watched as well.

The father, with one look over at his daughter and his smiling wife, said 'yes' and there and then turned and led Mr Sutcliffe to his study. Without preliminaries the father poured two glasses of port immediately turned to give Mr Sutcliffe his answer with delight.

During the prenuptial months amid all the excitement of dresses to buy and make, nieces to be trained as bridesmaids, the latest fashion in marriage in the new town, a large procession up the aisle of the church, it was a problem for Julia not to touch him as intimately as she wished to do. Her mother saw this and it made Mr Sutcliffe struggle with his own longing for her.

When she would go to the door with him to say goodnight she would feel her whole body respond to him, she was not a virgin, it occurred to her she was almost deceiving him but the longing was uppermost in her thoughts so she pulled at her husband's hand and he willingly followed and in the darkened room their bodies seemed to control them and they twisted together, their whole bodies touching as she felt herself reopened with her whole self. His need was as great as hers. Eventually he had the sense to pull away and help her to sit down and recover in a chair – somehow they managed to stop and with a whisper of, "Only two weeks," he was gone – she was a young 'virgin' who he loved very much and who seemed to really love him personally.

Because of the times that she lived in, she knew she could not have told him of her experiences and of her tremendous loss; but would she later be able to tell him? What if she could not give him the child that he longed for? Floods of tears came in her remorse and worry as she sat there trying to recover – she had to go back in and be sociable.

For his part, he was amazed but touched as he waited for his horse to be brought to the front by the flustered groom. He was touched by her obvious passion for him and resolved to stay busy for the short time yet until he was married.

And they were married on a beautiful summery day at the nearby village church by the parson who was an acquaintance of her husband; he had conducted the funeral for Albert's first wife.

Her greatest fear, though she could tell no one, was about the wedding night; that what should be a 'nervous bride time' with his own experience a doubt would be sown, because of course she had a lot of experiences, but he did not know that.

Would he notice, by her inevitable response to him, that she knew so much? That her lack of innocence might be all too apparent?

Would he wonder that she knew so much or that she could respond so easily as on that evening when she had pulled him into the darkened room? Would there be physical signs in her that would surprise him? How could she possibly know all this? That evening had surely been a giveaway. She knew that, although so young, she had felt she loved Mathew and in her inexperience had responded too much to his sorrow about his family which had led to the tragedy of an unwanted, unrecognized and unknown child. Their loving in the circumstances had been erotic and wild – she longed for that again. She did not know and probably would never know where the first love of her life and the father of her first child was. Neither did she know where her son was or if he was loved and well cared for.

Quietly living with such sorrow had matured her which was part of the attraction her future husband instinctively felt for her and loved about her.

Chapter 9

Jack Gains a Family

Breakfast in bed – Jack stares in embarrassment. This maid was the pretty one and the older one who sang was with her. They both got him sat up in bed with much laughter, which took some of the sting out of his embarrassment. The older one, he discovered, was called Nancy and the pretty one was called Dot for Dorothy or more often Dottie for affection. They had presented him with bacon and eggs and new baked bread with what he could see was a pot of strawberry jam. It was all on a wooden tray with what he could see was an embroidered cloth and on the side was a starched white 'log' bit of material wrapped in a silver ring.

"Wait," Dot said bemused. He stared. "Try some eggs, your napkin." Her pretty fingers unfurled the white thing and she gently put it up to his neck, tucking it daintily into the top of his nightshirt. Why was he such a bad boy that he looked to see if the drink was ale? It was fruit juice.

The older maid would later whisper to the housekeeper that pretty Dottie made him a good companion maid rather than an intimate nurse maid as it was a little too much for the young lad who had had such adjustments to make in his circumstances in a few days.

Mary, the parson's wife, decided they would see if Mistress Potts could find them a suitable young man as nurse to Jack, if and when more illness came.

Jack ate what he could and drank more milk. Was this the day they sent him for his new gardening job? He knew that he felt a lot better; his sore place was less fractious with its ointment and lint covering, but he felt worried. Where would he sleep tonight? It was getting so cold, could he creep back into this house or the sweep's cottage? He fingered his warm sheet gingerly, life could snatch them back he knew and put him back on the sacking.

He tried to find out.

"Oh, no," Nancy said.

They were going to try to build his health back up first here at the parsonage. He did not notice that she was rather fiddling with things with her back to him. She did not want him to see her sudden tears, she was a mother herself and it had gone round the servants that there was eventually probably not a lot of hope for the boy and that they must all act with some discretion and tact.

"I'm going to have another look at that sore when you have had a wash and then you can choose what to wear from that pile of clothes on that chair there." Jack looked at the chair and saw a neat pile of young man's clothes. He could not speak, were they really for him? He looked past her, he could see fields through the clean bright window pane, it was a little overcast but as he stared he could see two lovely black and white horses. It looked like a mother and a colt, he wondered how Jessie was back at the cottage, and what of Sarah?

He declined another embarrassing bath but was pleased that Nancy redressed the sore with fresh ointment and lint; it looked better. There were more snatches of bawdy songs and then she helped him choose from his pile of clean clothes.

The clothes were the best and warmest he had ever seen or worn, now he looked rather more like the thin but rather handsome young man he was meant to be.

Later, he met the parson's two sons, they were older than him – Mark and John; they loved horses and said they looked after the two in the field opposite the house. He could see that Mark was rather shy, like he himself was, so a friendship began to form.

Although his ragged hair had had a bit of a wash in the bath yesterday, it really needed some trimming and untangling. It was the family's gardener that came in to do this. He was like Nancy, with a ready smile and wit and Jack discovered he was Nancy's husband, like her he did not make any embarrassing fuss and she entertained them with some songs while he quickly cut back some of the curls and then suggested that he trim Jack's nails, "As there were all these pretty girls around," he said, with a wink and a shake of his head in his wife's direction and while he was there, as was the fashion for young men, he winked at Jack as the pretty maid popped in.

Then they found him some boots and suggested he might like to come downstairs for a while and perhaps have a walk over to Mark's horses, 'to be introduced', his limp seemed a lot better. And Nancy's husband said he might need a bit of a shave as was the fashion with handsome young men.

Jack found himself constantly smiling, he did not know this but the parsonage had now become his home and support system for his illness with the family and staff all willingly playing a part. The Weavers had four children, John the eldest and Mark and then the two daughters, Ruth and Emma, who were rather shy of him.

Somehow in the midst of such warmth and kindness his pain and his limp and his loneliness all got much better.

What also made the pain better was that Doctor Potts had sent some medicine over that was given to Jack regularly by mouth to take the sting out of his wound. This was appropriately small doses of a tincture of opium, for his comfort. The first two days had now slipped by and he spent some of the afternoon in the parlour that he had rigidly sat in on the Sunday but he was now comfortingly nearer the fire.

This second night had slipped by into another night but he was rather relieved that a maid just now was there for him if he needed her, outside the bedroom door, which was left ajar it was less embarrassing.

A middle-aged man came in to meet him on the afternoon of the fourth day. It seemed he was the one to help him alongside Nancy with bathing and tidying until the time when he was better, and could, 'do it himself' they said , keep that wound nice and clean, but Jack was so relieved to still have Nancy. The man was called James.

By this fourth day he did feel he was a lot better and he was showing a little colour in his cheeks, especially with the pretty maid Dottie, as James and Mark teased him about taking him with them to see and look after the two horses.

Jack was formally introduced to Molly the mare and her son. Jack helped them to eat a lot of apples just as he had helped Jessie when he could. Perhaps they would let him look after the horses? When he was better, his dream job was a stable lad. The colt was a little too nervous for him to be able to touch – the boys came every day now to lean on the gate. What should they call the colt they asked him? That day he had some dinner with the family downstairs. He was so nervous that the parson's wife thought he might be better eating in the kitchen than with the family, although as a family they did not stand on too much ceremony. But the parson would not hear of it. A family was needed by Jack and something of a family he would now have and the parson and his family watched Jack flourish for a while in his new home, ill as he was.

Chapter 10

The Final Part of Jack's Life

Several weeks passed and the nights were drawing in. Every day James or one of the boys, Mark or John, would walk with him to see the mare and her colt. He did not notice himself that every so often he had to stop for breath on the way but they all did, getting round it by making excuses to stop, pointing out sheep on a hill or the beauty of the November trees. When they got back, one of them would go to the study to tell the parson of how things were. Doctor Potts was guiding them saying that there would be increasing weakness.

Dottie was his favourite but he was very shy of her; she loved to sit to chat usually with Nancy to join in with the banter, but Jack would say very little just taking quick looks at his favourite. Nancy was gradually teaching him her cheeky songs, she was also the wound dressing specialist, together with Mrs Weaver. Sometimes the doctor would occasionally stroll in for a look while they were doing the dressing after Jack's bath; Jack had lost some of his shyness of the doctor who sometimes now brought his eldest son in with him, also called Jack, who was studying in London to be a doctor, like his father.

He was someone who also liked to come and sit with his namesake young Jack and they would talk about how young Jack had coped with such a difficult trade, the dark spaces and all that dust. Jack asked young Jack if he had often been hungry as he worked. As they talked young Jack was reminded of those times but somehow the memory was hazy because he was never hungry now. He did, however, remember the hunger pangs as the work wore on.

Young Jack loved to be visited by the medical student and to talk of London, the lights, the carriages, the royal palaces and the processions. Young Jack got lost in his imagination with images of so many people crowded into the famous, busy place.

He was reminded he seemed to have lost his wish for ale, he never seemed to get that now; it was water, milk or fruit juice. They did offer him a new hot drink they all seemed to like, calling it tea; apparently it was expensive and sometimes he was given sips of what they called coffee and Jack would tell young Jack of the popular coffee houses springing up in London. The housekeeper would take him through to the kitchen to show him tea leaves and coffee grounds. He took these opportunities to sit, this was his favourite place. He imagined himself when he was a full-grown man with his own cottage and wife having a cosy kitchen like this. This gradually became part of James's routine to get him down to sit in the kitchen for a morning drink.

So often he had more food than he could manage and he would struggle a bit; he hated to waste their food especially as nobody seemed to talk about him going to start the gardening job. He whispered to the pretty maid, asking her if he could have a little less on his plate each time.

But it was Sarah who was the real treasured visitor now each Sunday. She came and sat with him and the family. He noticed that her face sometimes looked so worried. He would try to whisper to her soon he would have the job so that she could visit him there, thinking she looked sad because she was uncomfortable and shy. It was quite nice for him that on Sundays the kind attention went from him to Sarah from the family.

Jack did not go to church but Sarah still did and would give him all the news of his friends. The family had found some new clothes for her too and she was looking prettier and more fashionable and Jack noticed that she would blush a lot when the medical student visited from next door.

The parson's family were trying to find Sarah an easier job at one of the big houses but they did not want to further aggravate the situation with the soot couple. There was a lot of gossip in the village and at the church, which was partly why the parson did not encourage Jack to attend as he would be stared at by everyone, "Wait till you are stronger." The parson had gradually introduced a scheme which was very relaxed and would see him saunter into Jack's room, at night to say some prayers with him from the prayer book running his fingers along the words for Jack to ostensibly begin to learn to read.

Sarah told Jack that a new climbing boy had come to work for the Soots but he did not live in, he lived with his family and she joked that he was quite a lot fatter and had cleaner clothes than the last boy. Master Soot had also invested in longer brushes; a lot of soot merchants were trying to do this, she said; she would often bite her lip now and look away from him out of the window with a troubled look.

Sarah knew that Jack was very ill with what people called 'soot wart,' some even whispered that this was a serious illness, she did not really understand words describing illnesses. She was just beginning to read more words than she knew, she often read with the parson's family on Sunday afternoons when Jack had a rest and then later John and Mark would walk her back to the cottage. Sarah had sent a message to Rose that Jack was ill; Rose was in fact a little jealous seeing

Sarah sometimes in the village in her new clothes with her glossy hair as she was eating so much better now.

Jack's cough had got a little worse so the parson or sometimes one of his sons would sit with him late into the night; and somebody would be allocated anyway to be on call each night. Nobody at the parsonage ever had to be asked to do anything for Jack twice, Jack was loved.

Nobody ever spoke to him about getting a job to pay his way, this preyed on his mind, he would whisper to Sarah about it and she would whisper back for him not to worry because they were quite a rich family and they were looking to settle them both in new situations in the new year she knew she was telling him very much a half-truth because her instinct told her that only she would be resettled. The evenings were drawing in as November passed.

The parson asked Sarah to come into the study as she was leaving to go home one Sunday and said, "I've been thinking Jack must be missing his friends from the church so a fortnight today I want his friends to come over for a parson style dinner. You can ask them next Sunday, if you would, and then they can come back here with you after church on the next; you can let me know the numbers, anything up to ten," he added with his hands curled around his cane this helped him think.

He did have this little plan that he was yet to tell his wife of, why not give Jack and Sarah and the friends a little party in the back room with the big table where they usually held meetings? The Weaver family could wait on them he thought, make it a bit of festive fun.

Mary, his wife, when she heard of his idea felt a small sense of panic that tested her faith, wondering how clean and well-behaved all these boys would be but the word party decided it for her, it was nearly Christmas – the day that the doctor thought Jack would not see.

The next Sunday, Sarah knocked on the study door, "Ten," she said bashfully. "All right, so it will be you and all of them round the table in the back room, with James as well, I think, and I am only telling you this – my children will help serve you." Then he looked more serious, "But our housekeeper will be in charge, do not tell Jack all these details just say some of his friends are coming to dinner and then let him tell you if he has any worries about it and you can tell me."

Rumours went round the house as the news spread on the Monday. Sarah had told Jack and they had quietly discussed it, they were both worried and excited at the same time.

The Sunday of merriment dawned – it was one of those bright sunny but cold days; and Jack had his bath with James and Nancy, they all watched the clock which Jack himself could read now. His friends would be waiting at the church now to get together to walk over. Sarah and Mary Weaver had sat with the boys before they left the church, and they had told them that Jack was pleased to see them but that he got quite tired easily and sometimes a little breathless, and did not often walk too much; and he loved to sit by a fire and listen to stories and so after the meal that is probably what they would do. If Jack was well enough they might like to go and see Jack's lovely horse and colt, the family had decided to call the colt Jack of which they were going to tell him about at the party.

The boys were all big-eyed with anticipation. Rumours had gone round the village so the boys were extra clean, the youngsters who were not able to be invited were a bit jealous but ten excited boys were enough.

On arrival, they all went into the kitchen where Jack proudly but shyly greeted them in his warm bright clothes and then James organised for them all to have drinks and some cake. They were all a bit, 'buttoned up' and polite especially when the parson himself came in to say 'hello'.

The kitchen was too full so Mark and John suggested they take a stroll to go over and see the mare with her colt. Jack had an extra arm to lean on surreptitiously and a tree trunk to sit on and apples to give his friends to give to the horses. The boys began to relax and run about and as Jack seemed content to watch them they spent a while there, the lads were encouraged to gossip and eye the maids, who themselves could not resist the party atmosphere.

Mary now wanted them to come in to dinner, it was an early Christmas dinner with paper chains and early sprigs of holly and candles; and Nancy was going to sing some carols, while her husband played his fiddle; she would throw in a few more bawdy songs later saying they were lads now.

Jack and James headed the table with Sarah at the other end, she had been upstairs to get dressed up with the help of Ruth and Emma. She looked the prettiest Jack had ever seen her look and knowing that she was rather fond of his namesake he hoped Jack Potts would be in to see them later.

Jack was too excited to eat much but they all did the staff proud and the parson's children enjoyed waiting on them, with John and Mark vying to be the head butler. John obviously had that bossy streak making him the best candidate.

James then judiciously encouraged Jack to take a little break after the meal before the music started and Jack Potts joined them upstairs, as did a now red-faced Sarah, looking her prettiest. After his rest, Nancy soon got to sing more carols and extra chairs were brought in for the maids to sit on and Jack found himself with Dottie on one side and the parson on the other. Sarah sat opposite with Jack next to her, both singing. Mary need not to have worried the boys had been spruced up for the party and they instinctively knew that their friend Jack was very ill just by looking at him; he was a shadow of the bright but shy boy that he had been, they behaved very well, it had to be said that all the lovely food had made them feel full and nice and relaxed.

Mary went out of the room as did Nancy when the friends crowded round to say goodbye; Dottie stayed in the room but stayed by the window knowing that this was a real goodbye and she thought her eyes might betray her.

***

As December came in they had musical evenings with the Potts family on the Saturdays and young Jack joined in well enough. They told him of their traditional Christmas party that they had in December, a lavish affair – no expenses spared. The children all made the decorations and entertained the guests with songs and carols and they practised a little drama that they would perform, a Christmas tableau.

They hoped to include Jack and had in fact brought the party date a little forwards but he could not now stand for too long at a time, his legs were weak and his ankles a little swollen at times. One of the men sometimes now carried him into the sitting room, he was very light in weight and he loved to lie back on a divan chair and watch all the activity around him. They made lemonade for him, it seemed to soothe his mouth and freshen it. If anything upset his stomach then student Jack often had an answer. As the party date drew near, Mary had a divan seat put next to the fire for him, near the corner so that he would be part of it but could snooze unobtrusively. He loved all the candles; but they let him be quiet if he wanted to be. He knew the carols from the church but here they were sung beautifully by the family that had let him become part of their circle. Some of the guests danced some jigs and did recitations.

The two chairs either side of Jack had a succession of companions while he dreamily stared at the party. For the first time his mind wandered a little, he wondered if his father and mother were guests. He had no memory of them of course but he gazed about himself just in case. He was sure he would recognise them, they must look a little like him, surely?

The family finished the festivities early and the guests drifted away; a lot of them approached and gently said goodnight. A friend of the parson and his wife came over and briefly sat with him telling him about their boys and how the parson had married them. She was a gentle and pretty lady and he gazed at her but she could see he wanted and probably needed to snooze. This was his evening and his Christmas, many of the party guests knew of the situation and would often later think of this boy and his story of being a climbing boy and of Doctor Potts who was such a part of their society by all accounts who did not approve of these young people being involved in such a trade.

Often now in bed upstairs they helped him to sit more upright in bed because then he could breathe more easily and he could still see his two horses, the mare and her son Jack – that always made him smile, the colt had his name. Do horses know when things are not going so well for us? They often seemed to come over to the fence nearest to the house, black and white and beautiful. 'Jack' was nearly as big as his mother and a lot more restless, cantering off to show them his steps and his swishing tail. Young Jack watched with delight. Sarah often spoke of Jessie, that she was quite a lot fatter now as the parson usually sent Sarah back with treats for the horse.

Sarah blushed as she told Jack that big Jack, as they called him, had walked back with her to the cottage the last Sunday; he had carried Jessie's treats, the parsons had noticed that Big Jack and Sarah had become fond of each other; Sarah did not tell Jack that halfway home he had asked her to sit for a bit, delaying their parting. Sarah had really blossomed, the food had improved where she lived as all the village eyes seemed to be on the Soots, they found themselves food for gossip for the village.

It was a week before Christmas, now Jack spent most of his time in bed – propped up comfortably with pillows. He had just been helped out to the toilet by James and Nancy, she was just about to give him – what she told the housekeeper looking rather professional about it – was a bed bath with nice warm towels; Nancy would only let James or the Mistress Weaver help her, Jack's limbs were very thin now, he just had changes of night shirts for his comfort. But his beloved pile of clothes were there on the chair next to him for 'when he would be better'.

Chapter 11

Looking Back to Julia's Wedding

Julia was a very beautiful bride, the whole village turned out for the spectacle of the very smart wedding of the people from the town, coupled with the beauty of the rural setting making it all seem perfect. Julia only looked at Albert shyly – even she was surprised how demure and unsophisticated she seemed and felt, especially as for the customs of the times at twenty-five she was a little older than the usual blushing bride.

Albert was a little surprised too at her downcast eyes, remembering their passionate embraces while they waited to be married. He squeezed her hand to distil the tension a little, both were feeling it, but for different reasons and both longed for the time when they could be alone and love each other physically, that is what they knew they both needed.

She knew she was enormously attracted to him. She could almost smell the pleasure she was feeling to at last not be so alone – but what appeared as such attractive shyness in her blushing cheek was really fear that she would not be able not to respond to him as explosively as she felt, she almost wanted to smile at herself that she was assumed to be a shy innocent maid. She remembered his erection against her thighs and how she had felt as they lost their balance together and she had felt such bliss as he found a chair for her in the half dark forcing her to be more sensible.

As she stood next to him now in her simple white muslin dress she knew she was stared at with desire in the eyes of the men. Her colour was bright and her eyes were full of her longing, as she felt aroused.

Afterwards, as arranged, together they walked back down out of the church full of smiles of congratulations and tears of relief from her mother and then they led the bridal party along the two lanes to the back of her father's house at the edge of the town where there would be a line of smiling servants to greet the bride before the reception and the guests came along. The village children had waited for this spectacle and played at the edges, throwing blossoms, the older village boys chasing after the girls at the side on the paths. Her two sisters followed first with their children then her parents, her mother squeezing her father's arm in relief – whatever is up with mother he thought to himself? A bit of overreaction he told himself, such a pretty girl was always going to get married.

She had taken rather longer than most, refusing many on the way that was all. Mother has got used to having her youngest at home for so long – he squeezed her arm back and smiled down at her he must remember to make a bit of a fuss of her over the next few weeks he decided.

Julia got through the wedding breakfast with her husband beside her, with his arm round her waist when they went to talk to the guests and with his soft kisses to her cheek; he did love her very much she knew that and she was longing for them to be alone so that she could respond. She wished he would just up her in his arms and carry her away.

She concentrated on just keeping her eyes down, really feeling wracked by her own desire, it had been so long and so difficult, perhaps eight years since she had felt the hand of love, she tried not to measure time from the year of the tragedy.

She must think of him, and what of him? Where was he? Would the child be eight or nine now? She always remembered his birthdays but counted them as little as she had been counting her own, who wanted to count years of loss and separation?

Finally after some dancing her father ordered his best carriage to take them the few miles to her new husband's house at the other side of town. Her sisters rushed forward they were relieved she was now settled, they had understood some of her shyness at the ceremony and the sadness. But Albert was a good kind man who would take care of her so they anticipated now that the three of them would soon be sharing motherhood and running households and the general problems of family happiness.

As Albert helped Julia into the carriage they were surrounded by well-wishers they held hands, Julia felt herself trembling; the carriage roof was down for discretion or because a shower threatened?

As they trotted away people saw them hungrily kissing and tut-tutted with a smile. Albert broke away smiling it had been so long for her, she lay back on the seat with her eyes closed, how many years? His mouth found hers again.

They both realised that they were getting near the house and broke apart. Both were flushed as they waited to be greeted by a line of servants, then they both separated shyly in front of their housekeeper to go for a wash and tidy in their own rooms. The housekeeper took Julia to show her proudly the newly redecorated room; blue, pink and mauve. Albert had shyly asked her favourite colours. She had known they were to have separate bedrooms; this had astonished her because her parents broke with the fashionable traditions of the wealthy and did not have separate rooms. Her father had a separate dressing room as an extra as well as a study and her mother had a sewing room and her own sitting room. Julia knew that her sisters followed the parental example exactly. She had not liked to say anything to Albert for seeming unseemly. Albert did not of course know of the family's unfashionable intimate traditions, beds and bedrooms for two which he knew had he known he would much prefer for them and in fact he meant to suggest it for later in their marriage. He had not wanted to shock his lovely lady, his virgin bride.

***

Julia sat on her bed, feeling a little flustered, she saw that she had an hour before they were to get back together for their first supper together as man and wife alone as a couple. She trembled with her turmoil of thoughts of how to get herself through until their bedtime, presumably alone on this bed. She had refused the help of her maid but she knew a maid would knock later to help her dress. She sat trying to calm herself. She slid off her wedding dress and lay on the bed in her bodice and petticoat trying to calm herself – then she heard a knock and jumped up and went over to call through the door to come later, "It's me." She heard his dear voice and without thinking opened the door just as she was. She did not know it but with her lovely face ablaze with longing, and quite a lot of fright of the unknown house and its procedures, she looked so gorgeous partly because she was so ruffled with her beautiful breasts more open to him and her hair slipping down over her shoulder. He felt unable to breathe but came in shutting the door– he just touched her face and then they were kissing and soon his hand and lips found her breasts and then he lifted her onto the bed and somehow some of their clothes came off and some did not and with minimal waiting now he entered her unable to wait- she cried out and he thought he had hurt her – his virgin bride. He had meant to take a long gentle time but she could not stop either.

Afterwards she found he was shaking and seemed remorseful thinking he had hurt her and he was trying to get her into the bed for rest when the maid knocked.

Laughing softly he grabbed some clothes and looked at her as she lay half in the bed and full of love and a tumble of curls. He went across to the door and looking back at his wife with a smile he called out that they had changed their plans and would have supper in an hour in his bedroom, on trays.

Then he turned back to his wife. They just looked at each other hardly believing how lovely it had been. He gently dropped the clothes aside knowing he wanted her again wanting to show her that he did and she edged the bed clothes off and slowly they came rather shyly together and they made love again more slowly and together and less shyly somehow.

Somehow later they managed to redress themselves of sorts, he was half dressed really and she had just a petticoat on, so she put a robe on top and he softly pushed it aside so that he could look at her curves and kiss her and then laughing he drew the robe across and pulled her though the door and along the passage – a maid did dart aside he thought. He led her into his own room seeing his own bed and sighed. He knew he wanted her there for the whole night and every night. He led her to the fireside chair and got her some wine. It was a half hour before the supper came and his longing was coming back.

She wanted to look round his room, he followed her, gently he lifted the robe off her so that he could see her and then he pushed her into a corner, this was incredible she knew he wanted to enter her again against the wall she cried out her joy. When they were calmer he took control, his lovely new wife he must look after her and he said get into my bed- it was not really wide enough for the two but he covered her up and found his own robe he was in charge he must sort these arrangements.

"I'll see to the maid," he said gently reluctantly covering her a little more, "I'm not sure I can let you go back to your own room tonight." He sat on the bed, "I want to sleep with you each night – I didn't like to tell you."

"My parents and sisters share a room."

He smiled and stood up trying not to be roused again, she would ache. His first wife had been so different. "I wish you had told me before or that I had asked you," he smiled. "Can I get a bed for the two of us after a respectful interval so as not to shock the servants?" This bed and the fireside rug would obviously be enough, he thought, for this lovely honeymoon time, they would share this phase of their love. *Two bodies always in love-making could cope with a single bed,* he thought, *for a while.*

"I must show you around the house," he said sleepily.

"Tomorrow" she murmured.

He was overwhelmed with his happiness, he had thought she would need enticing and some 'tutoring'. It was beginning to become apparent to him that he had had the luck to marry a woman who seemed to love to make love.

After their supper for which neither wanted much and both were a little embarrassed with the maid who brought it – who was herself blushing – Julia went and sat on his bed. The haste with which she had put on her dress meant that her lovely bust was tempting him again, he wanted to explore all of her but was worried that she was tired now. She got up to help him pull of his jacket, he was such a strong good-looking man, he put his hands on her turning her to pull off the sash of her dress, whirling her round and then she pressed against him unable to stay away, and somehow he had raised her skirts and they were back lying together.

The memories of these last years after his first wife had died went into his lovemaking he was amazed to find in the night when he woke she was on top of him in the night and he realised looking back how his loving life with that first wife had not been what he had thought.

They lay together satiated in the morning only stirring when two maids, this time both blushing, brought in their breakfast. He had been so sure it would take weeks to help her to relax and here they were wanton; probably the giggling talk of the kitchen below. In and out of each other's rooms each night making the servants whisper when out of earshot.

They also seemed to make love so naturally and she was immediately pregnant, they were both a little startled by this though so happy about it but would they be able to continue with such a pace of loving?

It did not seem to do any damage so the love story went on. This was the happiest time of their lives, for both of them.

Albert had a loving, exciting, beautiful wife with a baby on the way. She had a lovely husband she adored, to love her and soon, when the baby boy, George, was born another quickly came, Jack. It had been Albert's father's name, when Albert had suggested the boy's name when they were happily discussing names and she knew her firstborn had been named after her father, she had turned quickly away, Albert had looked at her as she had blushed, hesitated and looked down, "If you are not happy I would never insist, we both have to like the name." Quickly she had gone over to cuddle him, "No, let's have Jack," but over his shoulder she had had her eyes tight shut.

The first boy George had been much fussed over, to the point where her mother accused her of spoiling the child but pouring out her love on to this baby did help in some ways to lift something of the ache that she always had lived with for her first born son Jack.

She also found herself guarding her children more than she perhaps otherwise would have. Nobody would take these away.

Because the parent's relationship was so happy and strong in the first few years of having a family they almost became a little unsociable and exclusive. "I haven't seen you two," their friends and relations would often say .It was as though both of them had had to make up for past unhappiness. Julia's best friend, Isobel, was determined to see more of her friend, never mind the love nest.

The reality is of course that great happiness does not and cannot last, there will always be those clouds to come as though life and chance always have to rebalance themselves.

Chapter 12

The Final Hours of Jack

It was the shortest day of the year, four days before Christmas and Jack's mind seemed to be wandering – he thought Nancy was his mother and asked for 'father', so Jack Potts purposely sat down in the chair next to the bed, next to Jack's treasured pile of clean, clothes and seemed to read a book to himself literally filling the space that a father would have, next to a dying son, he hoped that is how young Jack would see it, if there were still lucid moments.

As 'father' he also spent most of the next day beside Jack. A Sunday, the parson had told the warden to bring Sarah straight to the house when she got to the church. Arriving at the parsonage she was shown in to the study; she knew what this must mean and burst into tears and Mary, who had not left the house yet, came in and sat with her as she was told Jack would not be with them for more than perhaps a day and that big Jack was sitting with him because young Jack seemed to think he was 'father' and that Nancy was upstairs with him as well, anxiously flitting about – the parson said with a wan smile – Jack thought she was probably his mother and she'd found it difficult to sit and take it so that his 'sister's' arrival would help them all and the parson quietly suggested the three 'important' people in sad young Jack's life could support each other for these last few hours.

Jack Potts was quietly reading to young Jack when Mary and Sarah went in; the lad did still seem to have some lucid moments. Young Jack lay on his side, he seemed to be following a story about a horse and Sarah realised it was Jessie in Jack's mind, she was pulling a cart and a boy was always giving her nose a rub.

The parsonage dogs had always rather scared Jack a little because he had been bitten by a black dog once when he had climbed out of a chimney but today there was a little puppy for him to look at, should he wish; it was still young enough to want to sleep and not be madly wanting to play, so Ruth and Emma would come and place it on the end of the bed snuggled near mum who was just beneath it with the other puppies.

Outside the sick room Jack did not know that the family were devastated, sitting quietly despite it being Christmas time; they realised they were waiting. It was because Jack was so young and dying of an illness that was not a natural one; and should be preventable, this caused them anger, bitterness and tears.

Jack stopped taking any fluids the day before Christmas and mercifully seemed to drift in and out of consciousness, bearing out Percival Pott's theory that these young men quietly and quickly die, because all of Jack's poor young body was affected now.

The parson had walked over with Sarah the previous Sunday and had suggested she could come over and stay with them for Christmas and stay through to Boxing Day. There would be young people there; the parson had already sent a ham that day to the Soot's house in order to be extra persuasive. The parson knew that the soot merchant had effectively caused Jack's illness but it was still the accepted trade practice to use climbing boys and there was a lot of competition for business so if they entertained Sarah over the Yuletide that might be a saving for the Soot's food bill – more ham for the two of them he thought grimly.

Jack was lying still when Sarah came in and she had already put her spare Christmas clothes in her room. She was excited even in these circumstances to have such a lovely room for the three days. Sarah did not own much but Mary had suggested that she bring everything that she would wish to keep; they thought they might have found her a better job as cook and housemaid to a widow who lived in a very pretty cottage in the village and the lady was very independent and active and Sarah could start in the New Year if she wanted to change. If she did, the parson planned to send a turkey with this information to the soot merchants that Sarah was sad because of the inevitable loss of Jack and would need a gentler job until she recovered and she would not be back.

It was now early on Christmas Eve and Sarah also would sit with Jack, who thought she was his sister. Mr Potts visited before his own family's festivities began that evening he knew that Jack, his son would be at the parsonage for much of Christmas. Mr Potts went in his friend's study for a chat because he knew these last hours could be traumatic and he wished to be called if he could be useful, although his son would be there to help.

Doctor Potts also wanted to enquire about the quiet girl who was like a sister to the boy. He had wondered if his eldest son was falling in love with her. He did not know what to make of it, the girl was obviously poor and of a different social class but she had certainly blossomed and was very caring and looked much better with Ruth and Emma's encouragement and fashion sense, but he knew she would be semi-literate and if marriage was a consideration – could such a girl cope with such a social leap especially one caused by such a very sad circumstance, the two had met because of Jack's illness. Potts knew that his son mixed with the intellectual and the usually rich young men while studying in London, the big smoke. That was another thing, the girl had really only known a rural setting.

The final moments thankfully turned out not to be as traumatic as they had feared, Jack seemed to rouse himself a little and he looked around him at what in that moment he thought was his family, Nancy, Jack and Sarah, and then he seemed to try to get up as if he thought someone from the window was beckoning to him to come and then he just breathed a little harder and imperceptibly his breathing stopped. It was soft, quiet... thankfully for them all.

After an hour and many sad tearful visitors they lay his emaciated body flat for the last rites and James and Nancy after a wash put on him one of his beloved flannel night shirts that now seemed so big for him. He lay with his hands together and one candle lit. Then practical Nancy with the tears so near to falling damped the fire and opened the window a little and between them they kept watch through that Christmas eve in twos, one each side of him through the night.

On Christmas night the boys carried him the short distance to the church in a cart with the mare and her son pulling him along and then the parson and the warden organised a rota of willing mourners to sit with him through the time until his funeral so that he would not be alone. The funeral was to be the day after Boxing Day.

Over the Christmas, especially during the day there were lots of visitors, the friends came in twos and threes and often were invited into the parsonage for a drink and some Christmas fruit cake.

It was always remembered as a quiet but prayerful and restful Christmas with few 'games' but more than usual poetry recitals and readings, there were still young people to entertain.

It seemed all the village came to the funeral except the soot merchants. The parson had been careful to send them a polite note when Jack died saying the parish would bear all the costs. He carefully sent a Christmas cake also thinking to carefully keep communication open; he knew they would be in a very difficult position in the village; some would blame them, perhaps they would have to move?

The parson had always thought of them as a rather sad couple without children of their own; they had been out of their depth with young Jack as they had tried to keep the business profitable. The parson did not tell his friend Potts any of this, Potts was always so angry about what he described as industrially caused diseases.

The mare from the parsonage was brought across with her frisky colt 'Jack' tied beside her to pull the cart the very short distance with Jack's wooden coffin to the grave- the parson had picked a beautiful plot to face the river. The mare wore a rosette and Mark had plaited her hair and tail with ribbon.

Mary and the warden looked after the boy mourners who followed Jack out of the church behind Sarah, the main mourner. The parson without asking his friend asked his friend's son Jack to walk with her; he himself was pleased about the growing fondness between the dead boy's, 'father' and 'sister'. This parson had little reverence for social class, he just saw people as people; as good or as 'in need of improvement', and this young couple were both extra good in his eyes.

Young Jack had grown up in poverty, largely an unwanted child he had contracted a difficult illness but he had had a great capacity for friendship and his short life had affected a lot of people, the parson had told the congregation. Nobody was sure of his age but Doctor Potts had calculated it as perhaps thirteen or fourteen? He had been developing further into manhood, despite such poor health.

The parson and Doctor Potts had a tombstone erected that read, "Young Jack a favourite of this parish."

Jack had finally found the love of a family. The soot merchants did soon move from the area.

Chapter 13

Jack's Mother Is a Mother

Julia soon got used to being a proper mother. She had had another baby on the way as her firstborn George was just going into the terrible twos. She recently had acquired an excellent new maid for the children; and as a personal maid to herself. She was a winsome lass, not pretty as Julia herself but a very kind and thoughtful person who was good with George and Jack, Julia had never been easy with her second son's name but it was Albert's preference and she could not or had not told him her history with this name.

Julia began to visit with neighbours soon after her second confinement sometimes with the children or sometimes she would leave them with Sarah. She felt herself to be something of an older mother as she was now approaching thirty; she did hope to have more children especially a daughter. Her sisters both had big families, but they had started their families a lot earlier. Of course nobody among their acquaintances knew of the reason that she probably married a little late but she, of course, had been the first daughter to have a baby, though nobody knew. She did feel herself to be quite popular in the area as an older mum and she and Albert were such an attractive couple socially and as parents.

She decided to take some more adventurous visits and took her children and Sarah to her Aunt Lisa's by the sea. Everybody enjoyed it especially promenading by the sea. Sarah in particular loved to promenade the children while Aunt Lisa thought she would give her niece a boost with a shopping trip to the local town.

They shopped in the lovely bright new dress shops and laughed at themselves in the latest fashion of hats, and then went to tea. Aunt Lisa was rather curious about Sarah and about Julia now that she was so obviously happily married and had her two children.

Aunt Lisa was always very direct and Julia had guessed that she wanted to talk to her about the past and its effect on her now that she had the two children. Julia felt nervous of acknowledging her painful past but was also longing to talk it all through with someone: her own mother and sisters absolutely never referred to the past.

There were rumours at Julia's house that Sarah was sometimes seen walking out with a young doctor who visited his parents in the village near Julia's parents' house. In normal events Julia now gave Sarah two days off- a weekday and the Sunday, after church usually. Julia often found herself worrying about Sarah in a way that perhaps Julia's mother Kitty should have perhaps worried about more; about herself and Mathew. Julia knew Sarah was deeply in love and had been probably for the year that she had already nearly spent in their house. Julia suspected there must be something of a social class problem. Julia knew the Potts a little socially, she seemed to remember going to a Christmas party at the parsons next door just after she had had her second child, Jack; it was a lovely party and she remembered talking to a member of the family who was very ill and he had said how he loved all the atmosphere with all the extra party candles. They had sat either side of him for a while by the fire. The young doctor's father, Doctor Potts was quite famous by now and had been knighted but was also a controversial figure in their local manufacturing town and its practices. Julia did not know a lot about all this but she did know that Sarah was rarely if ever invited to the Potts' home. Sarah often spent time with her sister Rose and apparently was very friendly with the parson's a family at the church where Julia and Albert had married, and Albert was a friend at the parsonage, too.

The young doctor she told Lisa over their tea seemed to be based in London and Julia with a confidential mischievous smile told Lisa she was thinking of taking Sarah and the children for a holiday in London next. Julia had always been careful not to ask too many direct questions of Sarah as she was her employer and also she could not confide in her the real reason that she really worried about her; perhaps one day she would confide in her she thought; Julia was now a bit circumspect with her aunt about it all. She realised how fond of her loud 'enthusiastic' aunt she was although she had been involved in Julia's tragedy, it had been very unwillingly.

Aunt Lisa was not about to give up, one afternoon when Sarah and the children were out happily overeating something locals called 'ice-cream', Lisa got Julia to sit in the garden with her and talk about the past. This felt so good for Julia, no one ever mentioned the past, her lost child and now the pain poured out of her. Her aunt watched Julia and wondered if she should go on and tell her what she had heard; it may only be gossip but Lisa did believe it.

Lisa sat and decided that she would.

"I think I should tell you, Julia." By now Julia looked as though she was nearly in tears, she looked so fragile. "There's a rumour that that milk nurse, Janet—" she found her hand involuntarily pointing at Julia and she quickly tucked her hands into her sleeves, "There was a rumour, that I heard, that the servants passed onto me, discreetly, that the eldest daughter, Elizabeth, I'm sure you met her?" Aunt Lisa in her nervousness felt she kept saying the wrong thing, stopping and starting. "I did hear that Elizabeth had moved to your town quite a while ago with her husband who had been a sailor and I think a bit of a drunk, they say they took the boy with them, they had no children themselves, that's why."

Julia's intake of breath stopped Lisa but she had to tell her the rest now.

"Apparently her husband did not come back from the sea, so Elizabeth found the boy a trade somewhere." Lisa had said it all now but she had not said 'probably sold'. Lisa felt bad but she had been right she thought. She had always wondered if Kitty, Julia's mother, had done the right thing, wishing she had not had a part in all of it herself.

Julia looked stunned, so was telling the truth really for the better? The aunt made herself busy pouring them some tea and glancing over at Julia's pale down-turned face. Lisa knew that in her heart she was crazily envisioning some kind of reconciliation for her niece and her firstborn.

Lisa had hoped to find out more; she was certain Elizabeth and Jack, if he was even still called Jack had moved the twenty miles to the same town as Julia but it was a large expanding, manufacturing town, but if Elizabeth was still there in the town perhaps she could be traced and some recent information gained. Lisa was a very realistic woman. Surely if Elizabeth was still really on her own, would she not be visible? Lisa knew Elizabeth would have to support herself and opportunities would be there in such a growing, expanding town. Lisa had never been as comfortably situated as her sister Kitty and knew the things women had to do in order to survive and support their children. What for instance she had often wondered would have happened to Julia if of the working class, like Elizabeth, would a husband with little money want to support an orphan child anyway especially if he wanted money for alcohol, like many a sailor she thought ;Aunt Lisa was not going to give up.

No Aunt Lisa was not about to give up. Lisa knew that children were sometimes sold to trade often as live-in workers. Lisa had women friends who had got involved with charities at the church who worked with the poor. She had told no one but always thought of her great nephew out there somewhere poor or abandoned or still comparatively safe with Elizabeth, who knew? She was wondering if she could trust a friend who worked in such a charity to help Julia and herself to make enquiries. Her niece was a very private person but with Sarah as such an excellent nursery nurse perhaps Julia could volunteer in her own town to see if she could get information. But there was such a probability of pain and failure. Lisa almost wanted to cry out against it all. It was all more than ten years ago now, at least. The boy if he had survived – of course he had survived she told herself, would be twelve or thirteen she thought. She had tried not to be exact about his age. She had never seen the child herself and now her niece had this lovely family but the pain was so visible about her, was there a solution?

The silence between them was not embarrassing or uncomfortable it was gradually soothing. Lisa had often thought her sister Kitty too ambitious and controlling but at least at the time the solution did seem to have solved the problem. But glancing across at the stricken face she knew her niece had a well-disguised broken heart.

For the rest of Julia's holiday by the sea this became a routine, Lisa and Julia talking and considering options trying to be hopeful, or settling on being resigned to everlasting loss.

Lisa, by the end of her niece's stay had settled that it might be best if through contacts she helped Julia trace an Elizabeth in Julia's town; with or without a boy Jack. If it cost them money they could contrive it between them and their housekeeping. Perhaps he was handsome and well, and a budding manufacturer?

Lisa worried had she made it all worse for her niece but she was glad the subject of such loss was now out in the open.

Julia went home planning to talk to her friend Isobel; she hoped she would be able to have her as a local confidante.

Chapter 14

Isobel

Isobel was a restoration woman loving the social changes and technologies that were beginning to appear. She also enjoyed being a young fashionable wife; especially going shopping. It was a joke in her wealthy social circle that her husband was thinking of putting an advert in the local paper: *Don't sell to my wife, she's a small, dark-haired lady in her late twenties who loves Indian fabrics.* Then, a little inebriated, her husband would spellbind the after dinner men's table with tales of how he would have to go into the local town to settle with irate but polite shop merchants using a 'link' boy with a flame for anonymity.

But he would never have the courage to tackle his wife himself face to face. Word had apparently gone round by infiltration and the shop ladies were asked politely to suggest that Isobel, ' think' about her purchases but she would never blame her husband and might then bring a little less back next time. All these stories made the couple great entertainment value in their society increasing their invitations while increasing the gossip.

But Isobel, to her husband's relief, at last formed a special relationship friendship with the most sensible of women Julia

Sutcliffe. They lived near each other and had met and got to know each other at afternoon tea parties in the town.

On this occasion Julia had Sarah with her so she sent her to do the shopping and the children were at home. They had enjoyed going into the new bright-looking shops that had sprung up in the centre of the town becoming what they all called the high street, but Julia had really come hoping to meet and befriend other mothers but eventually the real friendship that she enjoyed was with Isobel. They had seemed not to have a lot in common at first because Isobel did not have her own children but she had the same brightness and irreverence for life that Julia loved to share with someone. Since she had had the children and when her husband was away following his business affairs she could feel at a bit of a loss for conversation.

Sarah was such a helpful maid and Julia also had a lot of help from her sisters and her parents but she knew she lacked a confidant.

Julia still had not told her husband of her past and he was so happily married with her in fact much more so than with his first wife who in comparison seemed to have lacked love and passion. Julia and Albert still had a wonderful sex life together and sometimes he would catch himself smiling at himself at how much and how often they loved each other.

It had happened when he had gone to see his friend the parson in the village where they had married who had commented he looked like the cat who had got the cream and Albert had found himself smiling the more. Julia was enormously tactile and they had not needed the fashionable two bedrooms as they always ended up in one room or the other. Albert found himself smiling again that she might be pregnant again which he dropped a little hint to the parson about; but of course he did not confide that it had been when he was fondling her breasts that they would seem more enlarged and tender and she would squeal and make them roll over into a new position he could not tell the parson all this.

Julia herself thought she might be pregnant again, she did not want to tell her husband yet in case she was wrong but if true the thought of a third, in fact a fourth pregnancy had made her much more thoughtful particularly when she was alone.

Her mother had not once talked of her tragedy, nor had her sisters; it was as though it had not happened.

Her friendship with Isobel meant that they met often and chatted several times a week as well as at social functions. Privately there, they would laugh about their husbands foibles, even compare their sex lives and laugh together – giggling like young girls really it did them both good.

Isobel then did confide in Julia that her twin sister had died falling from a horse when they were young. Julia wanted to confide in her friend her own tragedy knowing instinctively that it would help her to confide in someone especially now that she had visited her aunt who lived by the sea and had had all those confidential talks and learnt all the gossip about Elizabeth and possibly of young Jack. Aunt Lisa of course had been an unwilling witness to the entire tragedy and was a very realistic person.

So Julia was certain that Elizabeth now lived in her own town and that Elizabeth who was childless had moved here with a young boy. Then there was the further gossip that Elizabeth's intemperate husband had left his 'family'.

Julia knew that Isobel had a wide set of acquaintances. And that she was well up on the latest gossip and because of her husband's business had lots of contact with the trades. Julia found herself thinking that Isobel might be the ideal person to try to trace Elizabeth and therefore they may get news of the boy Jack.

Julia did not intend to interfere and knew she could not, even if she did manage to trace her firstborn. Such contact or interference could be so damaging to so many people and what would be gained from it? Yet, romantically, she thought if she found him could she help him surreptitiously?

Her Aunt Lisa had horrified her by saying there was a rumour that Elizabeth and her husband may no longer be together and may now be impoverished and may – her aunt had looked away here – have sold the child to a merchant for money for the survival of all of them. Julia had been unable to look up at her aunt after she heard this however gently she had been told. It is one thing to think your child is safe and well and looked after if they are not with you but now she had to cope with this new development that he may not be, especially if he had been sold to an employer; how could she cope with such news of her son past puberty now very nearly a full-grown man? He may not be well or well-treated by his employer? Many merchants were notorious for not paying their assistants and not feeding them properly.

She tried to think of all the merchants that she knew who employed young men; only she and Aunt Lisa ever even tried to work out Jack's age. Julia thought of coal merchants and the soot merchant, as the town was now so prosperous for the moneyed class many were needed and they were very competitive. Her Aunt Lisa thinking to spare her niece further pain had led the conversation to brighter things that is when Julia realised she must have her own confidant, an informed local friendly lady, perhaps a friend of ladies' welfare committees who would understand and share with her to try to work out if anything could be done.

She would even pretend she approved of the use of climbing boys for the fashionable large chimneys. She was very well aware of the current debate among her class, some thinking use of such boys was essential and others who opposed it as a health hazard for the poor. One lady had lent forward and said, "Do try and get one who has a boy because they can climb and really get the whole fireplace clear inside and out." The lady had noticed how immediately pale Julia had become and all the other ladies had begun to fuss, offering her their smelling salts. Julia had quietly excused herself knowing that they would be gossiping as to whether or not she was pregnant again. Little did they know she might indeed be pregnant again, *not for the third time, but for the fourth time*, thought Julia, inconsolably.

These afternoon chats with these well-to-do ladies were painful at times but she knew there was not really any other way for her to try to gather information – within weeks she had a lot of knowledge of the coal and soot merchants of the area.

It was Isobel who in fact jokingly brought this up saying, "Have you got enough sweeps to choose from now?" Julia had laughed herself, not confident she could speak much just then. Isobel had recently confided in her that she thought she may now be unable to have children while of course Julia knew she may be pregnant for a third or fourth time. So she then decided that this may be the opportunity to confide in her friend and once they were alone she just blurted it out to a very shocked Isobel – the tale of the lovely Mathew and the illicit love that they had shared, just that once, and the terrible consequences for Julia and Jack and perhaps for Mathew, who knew?

Julia went on to tell Isobel there might be a woman called Elizabeth who had moved here to their town who may have brought Jack with her but the husband, according to gossip had left for the sea so that Elizabeth may have sold the boy to a merchant? He could even now be a climbing boy? Julia's face crumbled as she said this to her friend.

Julia then sat in silence realising that they were all as a family small and rather delicate to look at, with fine bones- her first real impression of what Jack might really look like, meanwhile Isobel was trying to take it all in; she was thinking of all the soot merchants there, all competing for trade- with their slim climbing boys often rather polite and angelic-looking and of small stature. Isobel and her husband had lived there for many years and seen many businesses expand and fail. She looked away a little and did not say that she knew of one who had had one such, who had quickly got very ill and had died. Isobel thought she might have seen the ill young man at a Christmas party, two years ago? Then she also thought hadn't Julia been there too? Isobel tried to think further and not dwell on this, but hadn't she seen Albert and Julia sitting talking to the boy? There had been a lot of gossip at the time because the parson had care for the boy and the famous Doctor Potts had been involved, a person in their own social circle who was known for his controversial interest and attempts at modifying the working conditions of these young labourers, the Potts family had all been at the party.

Isobel sensibly knew that she could not tell Julia of all these thoughts, of all this immediately or perhaps ever? She went across and just hugged her weeping friend and resolved to try to surreptitiously find out names etc. and dates.

Isobel later left her friend's house in great sorrow for her friend because it did seem to her that the trail may indeed lead to that poor young man who had died; was it a year ago last Christmas? How was she seemingly unable to have children and here her good friend Julia had been separated from her firstborn and the child had then very definitely descended the social ladder to the servant class even to the poor class who may, according to the beliefs of Dr Potts, have died from a disease directly caused by his employment as a poor orphan?

She did believe the doctor that all the soot and dirt may cause that sad cancer illness; she had heard that the doctor was becoming famous for his medical writing on these health problems of manufacturing.

Isobel found herself weeping as she went home in her carriage after her talk with her sad friend; she wept for herself for her friend and most of all for that sad young man. She resolved that she would go alone the next day to visit that village church that the gossips had all spoken of and where she did sometimes worship herself but tomorrow she would do a quiet tour of the graveyard. Julia had dropped the poor boy's name into the conversation it was or had been Jack. Isobel found herself needing to know and she knew thus Julia would soon know herself.

Chapter 15

Julia Thinks What to Do

Now that Julia knows of Elizabeth's move to her own town with Jack she cannot help thinking about the past years, for how many years would he have been living near her? It was all these unknowns that troubled her so much. Had they been at that village church to the same service? The thought appalled her, of those village children who had lined the lanes after their wedding at that church – the young men chasing the girls as she and Albert walked the two lanes to the reception at her father's house.

All those times she had visited her parents since they came to live here – passing carts; knowing her mother had the, 'sweeps' in that day, seeing the poorer boys in the streets on their Sundays off. Then she thought how she knew of many clerks in the town with children, some in school. But Jack had been sold, she thought. Some children she knew went to school for a few hours and then to work as well in the mines, she shuddered. A woman with a child who was not a widow would have stood out surely? Julia was spending a lot of time thinking and looking into space. Albert and Sarah were a little worried about her.

But it was Isobel who had the surest information for her, and Isobel knew that she must tell her friend without delay because all doubts seemed to have faded. She chose her moment Julia had just told her she was sure she was pregnant squeezing Isobel's hand and Isobel thought; *right time or not, Julia must be told during the early part of the pregnancy.* This surely was better than later in the pregnancy?

"I'm afraid I think I may know which soot merchant had looked after Jack." Isobel had spoken quickly and rather nervously saying, 'looked after' mistakenly because he probably had not been looked after and she was also aware that she had used the past tense because in fact of course she knew why she had – the boy was dead.

Julia was startled as she poured them their tea, she concentrated on that lovely smell, tea was their luxury, kept in a wooden cask that Albert did insist he keep locked, why was she thinking about tea leaves now? She must go and sit down.

She did go and sit down and they stared at each other; it had been the solemnity in Isobel's voice that had made her think laterally to tea. It had only been weeks since she had told Isobel and perhaps the past tense of the information Isobel was about to expand on had penetrated her thoughts and she was now in something of a shocked state. Her eyes were huge with foreboding as she stared at her friend and Isobel had turned pale this was the hardest thing she had ever had to say to anyone. She was known as rather a frivolous person but there was a great depth to her character she allowed few to see due to her twin sister's sudden death, she would need all the strength of character she possessed now.

Isobel drank some of her tea carefully giving Julia some time to try to think, she also went across to Sarah who had come in to check on instructions about the children. Sarah looked across at her mistress seeing that she was upset and Isobel suggested to the maid that they needed a little time to talk. She realised as she turned to give a little wave to Sarah as she left how useful Sarah would be to her mistress in the next few weeks and months, Isobel thought how much Sarah would be needed.

When the tea was replenished and they were alone again Isobel realised that she was stalling but for Julia not to know would be worse so now without preamble she broke the bad news.

"I think it may have been the soot merchant near your father's side of town," as she said this she knew Julia would have seen the soot merchant in the area and indeed her parents may have used his services. Isobel involuntarily shuddered.

"And I am afraid, Julia, the boy who it might have been," she tried to pause but Julia's intense look drove her on, "I'm afraid he did die." Julia's head went down into her hands; "but I think Dr Potts did look after him and I think the parson himself did take him in because he looked so ill." Isobel rushed on to say everything and said the wrong things but surely there were no right things to say? Julia had lost her firstborn twice: the first time she was too young to do anything else and the second time she did not even know.

Isobel stopped, her friend was now sobbing; this was not the time to tell her the dead boy was probably buried in the graveyard of that pretty church where in fact she knew Julia and Albert had married nearly five years ago.

Isobel knew there were no words for this moment, just the comfort of a friend and it helped Julia that her friend had been so bereaved herself in her childhood because she understood the impact of the death of a child to a parent in whatever circumstances- Isobel's mother had never really recovered. This was a newly bereaved mother of a son who she had not ever really ever been allowed to see and who in this life she would never see now. She had lost her son in birth and now she had lost him in death.

A further thing that Isobel did not say was that yesterday on the pretext of having left a glove in the church which she had specifically attended, she had visually searched out the parson and his family and the doctor and his family; particularly the doctor's eldest son who she realised she knew by sight and who was said to be in love with the maid, Sarah. She had, in fact, met many of them before. She also went because she knew the church was known for its friendliness and atmosphere. As she stood there that Sunday, the servant boys caught her eye; they were sat as a group being looked after by the warden and the parson's wife. They all looked relatively clean in their Sunday clothes. She was reminded how she wanted a child so much and thought could she have one of these often unwanted children? But of course she realised her own high social circle would not sanction such a way for her to become a mother; the higher, 'echelons' of society did not sanction adopting children but she was a rebel wasn't she?

She had not left a glove, but the next day Isobel had herself driven out and swept into the entrance of the church startling the warden who bowed low and she just said she was having a look without further explanation and as the man hurriedly said should he call the parson she said no she would just take some air and while the warden stood indecisively by, she went – swept out past him and sauntered into the grave area where she saw Jack's grave and went on past it turning her head away and then back past it again, and yet again – realising her friend would be utterly devastated by the new grief on top of the old grief and that such deep grief never really heals. Who usually had the misfortune to lose the same child twice? The thought of her twin and the sorrow of her parents reminded her, the loss of any child is the greatest of all grief.

Chapter 16

The Grave

Julia knew she had three things she must do; she would visit the parson and see if she should have a private talk with him, if she had the courage, and she must visit the grave and see Doctor Potts eventually if she could.

She thought she could visit the grave by being circumspect, she knew her parents went to the church in the town so she planned to go to the village church for two Sundays, perhaps not consecutively then she would then look a little more familiar in the parish and then could be seen to call there occasionally in the week. Once she had seen the grave she would call on the parson's wife.

So after a tense week, the next Saturday she told her husband she would be going to the village church the next day, smiling at him rather than explaining. Thinking that she was pregnant and might be behaving a little out of sorts Albert smiled back. It was the church they had married in, perhaps she felt nostalgic? She ordered the second carriage for herself and suggested their sons went with her husband to their usual church with Sarah and she hinted that there was a reason, a service she wanted to do for a friend in trouble? Isobel? She gave the impression it might be Isobel, she knew that Isobel would not mind as she was involved anyway. It would soon be dealt with anyway she wondered and wished that she could just tell Albert at this very minute but her instinct told her it would be better done later. She was certain now that she was pregnant; when she had seen her son's grave she would tell Albert the good news and the bad.

She avoided it for now. Albert did think she looked rather paler than usual but assented they go to the different churches. Julia got a lot out of her women friendships Albert thought.

So she went alone to the village church smiling at but not recognising anyone; she sat stiffly taking a look at the trade boys in their poor but clean clothes and after the service, with a polite glance at the parson she went quickly down the path and now it hit her that she had been sitting in the church where Jack would have sat every week.

The next Sunday she was careful to hint that she had a little nausea perhaps hinting at good news and so her husband left her alone; she would tell her husband later that her friend would only be a bother to them the once more and then she would be back with the family at their own church. He smiled and catching her round the waist said did she feel better? He treated her even more tenderly than usual. He hoped it was very much good news, and left her to rest before the service, then she went again to the church.

She knew she may have walked near her son's grave twice now or more times, she knew that this was where her dead son, her firstborn was buried.

She chose a weekday and telling Sarah she was meeting a friend at the village church she asked for the gig and also asked for the stable lad saying that she did not want to draw attention to her friend with a grand arrival; she was a little mysterious about it all.

Julia took with her some lunch for the stable lad who she preferred to drive her and encouraged him to let the pony graze on the green, and she walked to the church. She went in through the church gate, it was all quiet; then she walked towards the graves keeping her veil down over her face. There were many older graves but soon there was one not as old as the many. "Jack the climbing boy," it said, "a loved boy of this parish" and this is what added to her shock, he had died on Christmas Eve last year. She had been living just seven miles away while he yet lived.

She had expected tears but not this torrent of years of sorrow. How long it went on she did not know, she had instinctively knelt and was covering her face and did not see or hear someone approach.

It was the parson, who had seen what had happened. He gently helped her up and without saying much gently walked her across to the parsonage where she was helped to sit in the same room where Jack had first sat, in the beginning when he had first met Doctor Potts. The parson's wife came in while someone went to tell the stable boy on the green to take the gig back home and to take a message that the mistress had felt a little unwell at the village parsonage and the parson or his wife would bring her home later when she had had some refreshments.

The parson had observed this well-dressed woman whom he thought he perhaps did recognise in tears by Jack's grave, touching the grave stone- holding on to it. No story was needed if she did not want to tell them anything. Then the parson knew no explanation was necessary, a bereaved sister or probably a mother was visiting the lost child's grave. His wife was used to dealing with distressed people and she did not ask the parson about it all now, she could talk it out with the parson later, confidentially if appropriate.

The parson thought that the two women would benefit from a man's absence for a while and went to ponder on what he thought had happened, that the world had separated a mother from her child.

"Would a mother forsake her own child" said the scripture, he often read that verse from the pulpit. Perhaps it was the world that created these unnatural schisms? This must be the mother? And how like his mother in looks the boy had been even when he was so ill; the large eyes the curls and the same profile and he thought from what he had seen the same gentle manner. Before Jack had died he had cried at times in those last few days thinking people – the older maid Nancy especially had been his mother. The parson knew that he ought to tell or would be asked to tell the lady the details of this very sad story of the death of the boy. He hoped he would be able to talk to Doctor Potts first, he had much greater experience of bereaved parents.

The parson thought there had been some progress locally about the climbing boys, probably partly due to the death of Jack, the local society seemed to be turning against the idea a little, and there was a move to get government legislation about an age requirement at the very least. The parson hated this feeling that he had now; that all was so far from well with the local people and all the unnecessary suffering that he saw. Eventually this bereaved mother might be a help to the doctor in working to prevent these poor usually orphaned children from dying from soot wart, a preventable disease and death.

But what could have happened? He thought that he might know already – a wealthy family with a pregnant young daughter and the solution to pass the child onto anonymity, the age-old but cruel solution.

Then the parson went back to the lady and his wife. He thought he had seen this lady before? Had he married her here? There was now some coffee and a little conversation between the ladies.

The parson sat down and noticing only two cups said, "You two have that coffee." In the confusion and heightened emotion they looked over at him and he smiled and his wife with a light laugh offered to get another cup.

"No, not to worry." And turning to the lady he said, 'Would you like to come back tomorrow, perhaps to have a talk?" he asked her. Some of the sorrow had subsided a little she was so like her son she must have been about the age when her son had died when it had all happened the parson thought quickly realising his wife may not know what this was all about which is partly why he thought perhaps tomorrow rather than further upset today might be better for all of them.

So he continued, "Mary, and you my dear, I think I may know something of what this is about but I think a little to eat and a rest tonight might be wise, what about coming back at this time tomorrow? I am going to see you back to town if that is all right? I'm afraid I sent the boy and the gig back with the message that you had felt a little unwell so that you have a good excuse to have a quiet evening," the lady nodded, already looking a little calmer. He went away to order a little bread and cake and let the ladies continue to comfort each other, to have a confidential talk as only women can do about a child.

Then he walked over to the church while they had something to eat and drink and a talk together. The parson walked across to Jack's grave and stood next to it and put a hand on the stone and thought how much easier it would be if there were more honesty in the world.

The parson patted the stone again and heard himself say, "It's all right, Jack, we will look after her for you."

Chapter 17

Julia Returns to the Parsonage.

Julia went back to the parsonage the next day. She'd been quite thoughtful – albeit through the evening. She had looked a little sad, making Albert want to love her. But Julia had refused to be loved, this was unusual – it had never happened before. At first Albert was troubled though not angry. Julia and Albert both knew that in those days women did not usually say 'no' to their husbands. He had wondered if she might be pregnant and he was so pleased he did not try to press her to oblige him. He longed for a daughter. He had noticed that her breasts had been very tender recently –he had contented himself by watching her while she slept, gently undoing her nightclothes that he may gaze at her beauty.

Julia was greeted at the parsonage door at the prearranged time, with a smile and some refreshments and then a little while later was led into the parson's study. She always felt rather quiet in herself whenever she came into the parsonage. This was hallowed ground to her – to be where she thought her son had walked and been looked after by these kind people.

The parson had been preparing what he would say to her. He was tempted to let her do all the talking. After all what could a parson and father of a family say to a woman who had discovered that the son that she had made, given birth to and then quickly lost while young herself had had a different life than she had hoped for him, a life of great suffering in fact a young death here in this house.

Should they talk of Sarah? One of the better parts of the story. He had thought that if Julia looked for him to lead the conversation – Sarah would be the very subject.

Julia had sat down, the parson leaned forward he did want to say things to her he found.

"Shall we talk about your maid, Sarah?

Julia nodded, "I think she really loved him – your son – like a sister would have." This was all so awkward, "I think she was four or five years older than Jack."

The parson again left a silence, "Jack was at the soot merchants first, I think he was glad when Sarah went to work there also, I think the house was a lot better and they formed a bond." Should he say that Sarah had looked after Jack – when his own mother had not?

"I see a lot more than they all think I see when I make my parish visits," he made a small joke of it. Julia smiled, unevenly.

"And then of course I see who is a servant and who is not by where they sit at church and by their dress clothes," he seemed to be saying all the wrong things, Jack had not been born into the servant class, he had been sold down into it. There was another silence. Julia simply wanted him to describe everything so that she could picture it all and draw comfort.

"He came here with the sweep," the parson plunged right back into the story knowing this woman needed it to be told, "He was already quite ill, I think, the autumn before the Christmas when he died." There he had referred to her son's death – he had bowed down – he plunged on, "we thought that Master Sweep knew that we did not approve of these boys climbing to clean, we thought he was an apprentice, I think he had been here before..." the parson was saying anything and everything he could think of.

He saw Julia had shivered then, with no real choice but to go on – that is what he now did.

"Our housekeeper realised that he had been made to climb." Julia flushed – her son born to prosperity – climbing a chimney and ill.

"Not far, or a lot, because we do not have those sort of chimney. So... the housekeeper intervened and called my wife and said that the boy looked unwell, they'd give him some cake – he loved the cart horse, your boy," the parson paused and looked away at the window...

"Yes," he cleared his throat – the pain he must be giving this mother, "they came back the next day to do the rest, he was not limping so bad that day." Julia flinched – her boy had been less bad than the day before, "and we arranged with the Potts next door, he or even his son Jack might just have a look at him—" he nearly said 'your son', again. "After church on the Sunday when they would be in clean clothes." This, about a boy who had been born to the best of everything.

The parson fiddled with his quill – remembering, as if he could forget – everybody's shock when they had seen his soot wart and how invasive it had already become as the boy was past puberty when the parson knew older boys with this illness did not do so well.

Sighing he went on, "Things got better for a while with bathing and ointments. I had been to tell Master Sweep that Jack would not be back," the parson had said her son's name – Jack, "and Sarah kept visiting with him here."

"One of my older maids, Nancy, really felt for him, she had her own son." Saying the wrong thing again, he knew, but there was no right thing to say in such circumstances – he should not have mentioned the maid's fondness – this woman had lost this son, she had in fact lost this son twice – once at his birth and now so recently.

"We encouraged him to join in with the family but he gradually weakened," he was talking to the mother whose own family had effectively rejected the baby boy.

To lighten things a little if he could – he pointed to the window and there were two horses in the nearest field, "We kept those all the time for him to see or to visit." Such a short time he thought – three months – a little over ten weeks really.

"Do you want me to continue with these details, ma'am?" She nodded, this was a brave woman. He stood up and went to the window and continued to speak to her, from there – with his back to her thereby not seeing the tears that dripped unbidden.

"We had a party and Nancy sang and her husband played the fiddle, that was the time when he had his friends round, the boys used to spend their Sundays together – he did not add, 'in all weathers', she probably knew a lot of these boys had to be out all day and often had nowhere to really go on a Sunday.

"Mr Potts eldest Jack got on well with him and used to read to him. I think that drew Sarah and Jack together myself, that's what I think." He did not say Jack had seemed to young Jack to be his father. He gazed out at the garden and quietly prayed for the real father – another pause.

"We hired a man called James to care for him," he wished he had not said 'lived' or 'bathing', these were parental concerns and this was a distraught mother. Mr Weaver knew she had two sons in her marriage.

"We had one of us sit with him or nearby at the... during the last week," surely this would soon be over, he hoped.

"Is it all right if I go on?" He kept his back to her.

"Yes," she managed to say.

"The doctor had warned us the end can be difficult." Julia had to know, this had been her son, "But God blessed us," the parson came and sat down again, he knew he had to be nearer to her. "He seemed to just sigh and stopped breathing."

Julia's head sank down on her arms on the desk and the parson came round to stand just with his hand on her shoulder – what had been needed had been done. Nothing more could ever probably hurt this woman as badly as this.

In a while he went to the door to signal to Mary to make some tea and to come in with it, herself; she understood and later the couple sat with the grieving woman, a mother too late to help her son.

Chapter 18

Good News and Bad

Julia realised after she had seen the parson how 'nervous' she had become and must seem to be. She had to tell her husband of the pregnancy, should she at the same time tell him of the past?

Should she tell Sarah first? Sarah was involved with the doctor's son she felt sure and was beginning to think Sarah must have known Jack because of her age and that she had lived in the village and would have attended the same church. That was another conversation she had to have. It was guesswork but did she not remember Sarah had been a maid to a soot merchant. Julia had lived for over ten years with the effects of secrecy and concealment. She knew now secrets and lies hurt people – she thought she saw the secrets caused by the love that Sarah had – was it damaging her? It probably was, Julia must talk to her husband and then to Sarah – she must bring things out into the open.

Sarah was in deep thought in the carriage as she, Sarah and George made their way home. Sarah was looking very well – she had caught the sun on her face and hands when they were at the seaside, and Julia thought when a woman is in love it does show.

George had fallen asleep with the motion of the carriage after a big dinner of meat pie and potato, which he loved – he was well over two now and talking endlessly, word after word – which he chuckled over.

Julia looked at Sarah across George wanting to pour out her heart to her. So she said, "We'll have a long talk in the week, Sarah, just the two of us, if you like, once we're all settled back in?" Sarah nodded, she loved the coach rides especially; she rode inside with George and his mother. She felt a little dreamy she was wearing her smart, new, blue dress Julia has bought for her. If Jack could meet her this Sunday she would wear the lovely pink outfit.

"I also wanted to tell you about other things, briefly for now, Sarah, because we are nearly home and I might have to wake him," she smiled down at George so still, in his lovely child's sleep.

"The first is can we talk about where you worked when you were growing up," Sarah snapped wide awake, a look of some worry now – the parson had arranged for her release from the soot's house, she had first lived as a companion to an old lady in the village learning something of a more genteel life and improving her reading, it was a lovely relaxing way of life but the parson guessed that two years after young Jack's death she needed more lively circumstances and when the lady died through his connections the parson got her appointed as Julia's maid which was now her dream job with a lovely room to herself, good food – the company and laughter of the other servants, a lovely naughty little boy and her two days off a week, and a baby and perhaps another on the way and Jack to love, whom she hoped to marry – she just a servant girl.

The two days off a week meant that she usually was able to meet up with Jack on one of them. Her future dream was some acceptance of her by his family, she longed to be invited to Sunday lunch at the Pott's house. She was well aware of the class difference; she fitted much more easily into the parson's house where class did not seem to matter.

Julia brought her back to reality with "and I am sure I am pregnant again. I think you had guessed." Sarah had been wondering. Sarah had been envious – now perhaps there would be another reason to stay in this job that she loved but there was a jolt – being in love – she longed for marriage and a baby herself.

They had a lovely chat about Julia's plans and Sarah began thinking could they all move to the great city of London where Jack was? All the talk of plans helped Julia who knew this was the evening she would tell her husband both of the good news, the baby to come, and of the baby lost, and the bad news, he must now be told.

George was a little bad-tempered on waking but his father had heard the carriage and came down to them. George found he was pleased to be home after all and went off chuckling with his father to fuss him.

Sarah helped Julia get settled then on impulse as it was a Saturday evening Julia said, "You can go now – go and show Rose those new dresses, take the pony and trap, say that I said and stay or come back in the trap if she cannot see you and go back in the trap tomorrow – we can manage at church without you.

And Sarah a little flushed now in anticipation and Julia then rather astonished her by saying, "I know you are walking out with Jack Potts," Julia was looking straight at her, Sarah blushed at a loss. What did she see? What the Potts family saw – a twentyish-year-old spinster with marriage ideas way beyond her station – which she knew to be something of the truth anyway.

"I am only telling you this first to wish you luck." Julia was supporting her – Sarah was dumbstruck, "No wait I am going to ask Dr Potts if I can see him as I am pregnant but also because I want to talk to him—" she hesitated, "about the climbing chimney boys that he is so active and anxious about."

Sarah was looking at her strangely and with sadness. "You go now, Sarah. We'll talk all about this on Tuesday, shall we?" Julia wanted to add, before your day off when you may be able to tell you – Jack her lost son, her Jack, his father figure during those terminal days would... might be... a real father.

"Can I also just say, I know there was a boy there called Jack as well at the sweep's. He died at the parson's house – no, Sarah, don't worry." Sarah looked so upset now. "We'll talk it out then, shall we? I know you knew the boy and was his friend, I have seen his grave – go and show Rose those lovely dresses." And she waved Sarah away. "I've got to tell my husband some news."

Julia wanted to steady herself and be alone. She wanted to check which of her beautiful dresses would suit her for this special meal; this was a difficult evening ahead.

Her husband burst in all smiles. "He's fractious but he is so tired he will sleep, he probably is already." And then his voice went low as he came to kiss her neck, her response in her heightened emotional state, after her talk with Sarah, was ardent and immediate. They made love ecstatically, he always missed her so much when she was away overnight.

Afterward they lay close, both so pleased that they could love each other so completely.

"Albert," she propped herself up, was this the baby moment? But he kissed her, silencing her, beginning to want her again. Gently she got up and went to the wardrobe to finger her dresses.

"Are we sleeping here, chez moi or chez vous?" It was their long-standing intimacy joke because it was ridiculous they had two rooms and only slept in one or the other.

"Dinner is in half an hour and I must look beautiful, I want to talk to you and I must say goodnight to George and baby." Albert left her after sex he always felt so relaxed. But he was wishing it was the old days when they would stay in bed with trays coming up from the kitchen and they would have 'between courses' but he went to say goodnight to newly bathed sleepy George and baby, again he thought was she pregnant again? Her breasts were so tender, *another lovely brother or sister for you*, he thought as he kissed his sons. He was something of a hands-on father for that time in history – the maids rather marvelled at it – most fathers from that class, in other houses – they would compare who they worked for, most fathers were hands-off strictly just overseeing their children from a lofty height and often rather grimly.

Julia and Albert had a quiet meal; they touched often both knowing it would be a night of lovemaking. She was wearing his favourite cream gown he noticed- it showed her beautiful curves and he kept losing his train of thought watching her breasts thinking they were even larger and lovelier – she knew he was watching her so lovingly and bent low – he came round to kiss her – she was embarrassed as servants still hovered so he said to them just bring the dessert and coffee together and leave us, we are both tired.

The servants were smiling too, 'too tired' really meant; enraptured with each other overnight, this was another difference the servants joked about – most mistresses were submissive and a lot of husbands seemed cold – living lives as married bachelors – not their Master and Mistress who seemed to live a romantic tryst of a life.

"I've good news and bad," she now said as they ate dessert and knew they would be alone. He took their coffee cups over to the small table beside the couch, Albert was wanting to make love again now as they were undisturbed.

She said, "It's important," and as he began to fondle her and shed and lift the heavy material of the dress, "I think I'm pregnant again." His joy was immense and immediate, in his excitement he kissed her and they both ended up on the floor laughing. He was so roused but suddenly nervous. "It's all right," she said and they made tender love again.

"Bad news – how can there be now?" he said in a muffled voice as he stroked her. "There is," she pulled her dress back over her bosom how could she tell him what he had to hear now – looking like a wanton strumpet? Perhaps her timing was wrong. He gently stopped her and kissed her breasts lovingly this was the part of her body that he always adored.

So she let him drowsily fondle her. "You are not going to like what I am going to tell you" – his hands were moving down longingly he wanted to cherish this special night.

"Please listen." He lay back on the rug and looked at her sensing this was important. She bent over him and he opened her dress to kiss her as he listened. "Albert, a long time before I met you when I was young I had a serious friendship with a boy called Mathew." The news was tumbling out now, "I was fifteen, I think, we made love just the once, we got lost in the garden in the moonlight – I got pregnant. Mother arranged for me to stay with Aunt Lisa – they took the boy straight away. I think I have traced him. I think he is dead.

The change in Albert's face and movements she would never forget. His face went hard and even a little cruel as he stared at her – sitting up as though he was not sure where he was or what to do. Then he seemed to gather himself together and without a word he got up, and without even looking at her he adjusted his clothes and left her.

She lay against the chair, in the firelight bewildered; she had got it all wrong. She was lost, and her heart broke for a second time all these years later – loss, loss, loss. Perhaps he would never be able to forgive her? Should she have told him before they were married? They had been so happy in their new love. Why had she thought he would be able to forgive such a thing – and go on living with her and loving her each night?

That was the first night in their married life that she slept alone. She had deceived him, he was in turmoil.

Chapter 19

Albert's Reaction

When Albert left her he could not think what to do so first he went to his room slamming the door before laying himself down – she had had another man and a child.

Unable to bear this line of thought he got up and grimly dressed in boots, cap and coat quickly and he astonished some of the servants still chatting before bedtime by thundering past them without a word and letting himself out of the front door. He would walk and walk.

A bit of him wanted to go and get his favourite horse and ride and ride but then he would have to disturb the stable boy and talk so he just set off down a path. There was some moonlight but he knew every inch of his land so he knew he was safe – he could have been blindfolded.

And that was exactly how he felt as he strode along – blinded – she had been with a man before he and she were married – just the once she had said – his name had been Mathew and his family had been ruined. He battered at any tree branch that got in his way with his stick. That she had said was a moonlit night – they had got lost in the garden in a rainstorm in their passion. He could see it all so clearly in his mind's eye as he hit out at the trees if they got in his way – young and beautiful Julia with a young man – who was in a shocked state about his family – as they made love unexpectedly and nervously, unable to stop she had hinted.

He now threw himself down under a tree and gazed up at the half moon – wishing he had thought to bring his hip flask – he could have poured it into himself to blow these images to something bearable. But he knew he had to think it all through, however painful and what about that 'given away boy' – away from his family and ancestry – how cruel the world could be.

Memories flooded back – he had fallen hopelessly with Julia at first sight – thinking because of their age difference and his bereavement he would not stand a chance – but he had become obsessed with her beauty and particularly her genuine smile and obvious wish to always chat to him – he had started to purposely make sure he went to all the social events she would be at. Her figure was exquisite and all the men or indeed a lot of them were wanting her as he did. But what the men had 'liked' about the unwed ladies of their acquaintance – over their after-dinner port and cigars there was always the same story – Julia so beautiful but to most men's taste rather a cold person – even if they could ever get her to love them back they said would there ever be that marvellous passion and warmth that all marriageable men dreamed of finding in a woman of their choice: good looks as well as passion were probably too much to ask. But... he got up and walked again, striding along – she had fallen in love with him and had astonished him with her immediate passion – and he remembered even before they married – she had wanted him; he hit out at more branches – was he now seeing the reason why? She longed so much for a man's embrace.

Soon after they met she had responded to him although he was older and a widower. Did her instinct tell her he would be used to the intimacy that she cared about above all else? She had looked straight into his eyes and when they danced she had trembled and they had consciously brushed against each other in something of the start of a sexual embrace.

After those first few dances together when he met her again if there was not to be any dancing he longed for the touch of a dance and would almost bump into her half consciously, they seemed to have an electric touch between them then, as they did now – he was walking across country now – oblivious to the cries of the startled wildlife in his path – beneath his fast pace.

The courting had been swift – the young men were a little jealous and put out that an older widower seemed to have so effectively breached her cool defences and successfully wooed her – they were well aware of the looks of love she often gave him, they became the subject of the town's gossips. And then he thought of that time when she had pulled him into the darkened room and he had been so obsessed he had nearly taken her – his erection against her – but he thought she was a virgin and it had been her parents' house and they could be disturbed by anybody. All these things had restrained him and he had to push her away into a chair and leave her. Should he have left her for good and broken off the engagement because her apparent lack of innocence had worried him – he had consoled himself at the time it was because she was that bit older for a marriageable woman and deeply in love with him – but now – what would he think? If he had known of the boy – would he have indeed walked away?

And then later at their lovely happy wedding he remembered her longing look and quick passion in their first days as a married couple, their constant lovemaking.

He sat down again, on a tree trunk finding himself weeping a little, so what did he as a man really want anyway? Innocence in a woman?

Yes, if possible, but most definitely a passionate response – he had what he wanted surely? A lovely wife who loved to couple with him that other men envied, two beautiful sons and possibly another one perhaps a daughter on the way.

So he walked and walked – what could he do, what did he deserve? A perfect life? Nobody had that, he had been wondering why his had seemed to be – his love for her now had changed but he found he did not love her any the less.

And the boy – the boy had died – he now had to sit down again – to absorb the enormity of this – so Julia would never see her firstborn again and he would never see the boy himself – this surely seemed like something of an answer, something of a solution?

But, the question remained – would he have married her knowing that she was not indeed the virgin that he thought she was? Effectively he had been deceived – should she have told him? He thought again of their wedding night her unbridled erotic reaction that he had assumed was based on her great love of him and of course it was – she did really love him he knew that. But looking back with what he knew now it was because she loved to make love with a man – that coldness that other men had found had been a reaction to her great loss – nothing had really changed for them as a couple? – But it had, he thought, hitting the ground with his stick.

She has borne another man's child – had given it away – she had not ran off with the child so as not to lose him had she? She then had not told her future husband and even now had only given him the vaguest information.

He felt he needed to know more details but did he? He remembered how it had been when he was young – how he longed to just make love to women so much on a couple of occasions he had visited prostitutes but had found that this transient sex did not really appeal to him. He had always been a romantic; he knew that is why, if he was honest with himself, he had fallen for pretty but frail Laura his first wife and had married in haste. He still had these painful memories of those first few months when she did not really want to have intimacy. How each night he had knocked at her bedroom door increasingly desperate and sometimes she would let him in to fondle her a little as he tried to persuade her.

Their 'love' had finally been consummated after some months. He had loved her and he thought she had loved him in her way but she never seemed to want much lovemaking. He remembered guiltily that soon she had fallen ill with a lot of chest problems and consumption was diagnosed, and there had followed the two painful years of her getting weaker and weaker and Albert looking after her. But he remembered the pain of the loss of their newfound intimacy his feelings of immense loneliness, frustration and some more visits to a high-class prostitute on occasion.

A year after Laura's death technically when he was still assumed to be in mourning – he had fallen deeply in love with Julia. The marriage and the honeymoon and since had been the happiest years of his life leading to the birth of two healthy sons.

He had walked and sat for such long periods that he saw dawn was beginning on the horizon and the birds were beginning to wake.

He made himself go home, startling a maid, they had taken in turns to wait up for him. The whole house had been worried – the maid brought him a hot drink – his wife – she could see was in her own room, not in his.

The maids would later tell of them sleeping in their own rooms for the first time and cook said it was inevitable – loving like that was not meant to last – you had to come back to earth sometime and live with consequences, as other people did.

Chapter 20

Julia Thinking and Alone

The morning after Julia had slept alone for the first time in her married life – she did not see Albert at all.

She soon noticed that the maids were being ridiculously polite to her and to each other, there was tension in the air. She found out that Sarah had stayed at her sisters so that she thought she must go out and she and George her eldest went to church alone together.

Isobel was there; who saw how strained her friend looked. Julia was preoccupied with her troubled thoughts, she hardly heard the service and George was so well behaved in their pew box – he only occasionally brought her his things for her to look at.

She noticed a lot of her social class did not bring the children to church or if they did they often brought a nursemaid so that there were no disturbances to distract the congregation.

Isobel played something of a nursemaid role giving George quiet attention, from the pew behind – realising something had happened to Julia.

Tossing and turning all night rather than sleeping, scared about so many things, her marriage, the new baby. It had all struck, as awful thoughts tend to do – in the night – that Jack had been living about seven or eight miles away, getting more ill, while she was enjoying being married and being a mother to her second born, George – Jack's half-brother – Julia's second baby, but not her first, as relatives and neighbours assumed – a new mum to everyone around her. It had been a lovely time for her despite all the deception – loving her husband and being loved so much, and the second boy had added to their happiness, her new Jack.

She was a new mother, the mistress of a lovely house and probably enjoying a joyous Christmastide that year that her firstborn lay dying. She remembered her long talk with the parson, learning and sharing dates where possible – learning of Jack's unhappiness and then his happiness due to being part of a loving family, for the very last part of his short life. That Sarah had faithfully come to see him in her 'role' of big sister.

Julia thought of all this, her mind in turmoil and thought of her visit to Aunt Lisa and beginning to search and now she was here alone in her room, longing for her husband, she could still see the pain and disbelief on his face. Albert was not with her and may never be again in her bed, perhaps not in her life as he had been- if his grim silence since was a clue.

She was probably now to be an unhappily married woman with a third and indeed fourth child on the way, although Albert may not know that.

After the service Julia took George back to Isobel's house. Julia was unable to really explain it all to her friend, it was too raw yet – but she did tell her she would see if she could see Dr Potts about both her pregnancy and her dear firstborn son Jack and even if possible talk to Dr Potts about his own son Jack and Julia's maid Sarah – who were clearly in love.

Isobel looked puzzled so Julia told her about her maid and Dr Potts' son, who Isobel knew a little. Isobel looked amazed Jack Potts was very much the gentry and Sarah was a servant. Julia nodded understanding the confusion if she could not get her own life better perhaps she could have the comfort of helping Sarah to find a happy outcome – what did social background matter if people found love; but she knew not everybody would agree – in fact most of her circle would definitely not agree.

***

Jack and Sarah were probably meeting that afternoon. Sarah was still unsure – but they met upon a certain place if it was sunny then they would walk and kiss and walk.

They knew that they did love each other but neither had put it into words the barriers so great.

That Sunday, Sarah was wearing her pink dress and matching bonnet and lace gloves – Julia was the best mistress. She did not see Jack until he touched her from behind – her face was on fire, they kissed hungrily – he had passed an exam and she had news of Julia's probable pregnancy and the holiday by the sea and talk of a holiday in London but neither said much yet.

The early autumn day was very sunny so they sat down together somehow they laid down. When this had happened before she gently stopped him and he stopped himself but because the day and the news were more intense he thought she would stop him and went on and then it was too late for him to stop himself – he had lifted her skirts and they were making love – afterwards she felt so wonderful but was too afraid to look at him. He was so relieved it had happened and wanted her again but lay next to her unable to speak. Then he did,

"Sarah, I think you know I love you – come to London with me tonight," and then they looked at each other , her face was pretty, lit by love and they made love again the first time ever for both of them such intimacy, each were astounded at such joy.

Julia saw a difference in Sarah immediately when she did return that evening. Sarah saw that there was a bad atmosphere the Master did not speak – she had nearly just left with Jack but something told her to be cautious. Jack had said he would tell his father when he got back, that Sarah and he were determined to marry and live together. Jack had looked at Sarah as she stood there shyly checking the lovely new pink outfit was straightened; he smiled and went down on his knee in their Sunday shelter.

"Sarah, will you marry me?"

There was not a yes just a squeal of joy and the dress got quickly un-straightened again as they kissed – he wanted to get back eager to tell his family if he could before he returned to London and Sarah to tell Julia and later Rose if she could, when she could – could she? She was a servant – servants did not do these things.

Julia prompted her, "Could I tell you something now, Sarah? The Master will not be in here tonight." Sarah stood there dazed with love, Julia was preoccupied. Trying to be calm. "I've a shock for you, Sarah," Sarah tried to bring herself back to the present and sat down with her Mistress to share in a confidence more as women friends than as Mistress and maid.

"Sarah, I'm sorry," Julia breathed in afraid. "I had a child when I was quite young, fifteen, I think, the family hushed it up and he was given away to the wet nurse's family."

Because Sarah had had such a lovely day making love for the first time – perhaps she had made a baby with Jack? She almost smiled and took Julia's hand. "Love happens so easily," she said kissing her mistress softly, and Julia knew that Jack and Sarah had made love themselves, Julia had to go on.

Holding hands she continued, "Sorry, Sarah, he was called Jack, my son." Sarah's dreamy eyes focused more sharply she drew in her breath – was it the same young Jack? They stared in silence at each other.

"He was your Jack – the daughter of the wet nurse Elizabeth was abandoned here in town and could no longer look after him." Julia and Sarah hugged each other in silence so much had happened today to take it all in – for either of them. There was so much to say but so much had happened – tears and snatches of sentences were all they could manage.

A few days later they would pour out their hearts to each other about the two Jacks in their lives – both loved and one lost.

Julia kissed Sarah and said, "Go to bed now, you won't lose your Jack, I lost mine, I could not bear it for you"

And for the second night she lay alone, deep in grief and pain.

Chapter 21

Julia Meets Mr Potts

Julia knew it would help her if she spoke to Mr Potts about Jack, she wanted to tell him that she would try and help him if she could by any social influence that she had to try to stop the practice of soot merchants using climbing boys.

Besides which she was very sure now that she was pregnant again and with her way of tempting fate she thought she could confide in Mr Potts. She hoped it would be a girl – she often had to resist telling Sarah she was definitely pregnant, she did not want to explain the marriage difficulties during the many woman to woman talks that they shared, even though they were Mistress and servant. She would be glad that if and when the marriage recovered she would be able to tell Albert that Sarah had known and befriended Jack.

The whole house was relatively upset now. It had been such a happy marriage and a relaxed family. Now the couple slept apart and barely seemed to speak; and if they did it was very politely. Sarah herself was rather quiet and worried about Julia and even more in love with her Jack now that they were lovers. They met where they could and when they could. They did not seem to understand the risks they were taking but the melting moments of their love were now so intense – one felt they could not live without the other.

Jack kept trying to tell his parents, of his plans to arrange for Sarah to come and live in London with him. He knew of the turmoil at Sarah's mistress's house and pieced two and two together about the origins of young Jack from all Sarah had told him. This was a future bond uniting them, their shared love for the dead boy for whom they both grieved.

Julia had seen the parson and her pregnancy was progressing well but the marriage was in an appalling state – but now she wanted to have a talk with Mr Potts himself if he would see her. She felt she needed to plough the depths of her sorrow, she was however determined not to be too emotional although the state of her 'baby moods' made that so difficult. She had confided in Sarah on the Tuesday that she might go to the Potts' house and would sort of 'announce' herself at the door uninvited as she was, perhaps the next Saturday. She knew Sarah might be seeing Jack on the Wednesday her day off, and she herself might bump into him on the Saturday at his house. She told her quiet withdrawn husband at the breakfast table on the Saturday as he arrived for his own breakfast purposely a little late. They tended these days to often just miss each other for meals – she said that she was meeting with a friend for lunch, 'another pregnant lady' that she knew – she threw this statement over her shoulder as she went. She was smarting from his anger and his neglect.

Albert turned away, he had found the last two weeks so difficult. She was wearing her yellow dress today, he loved to see her wear it. He turned away so as not to let himself bury himself in her arms if she would have him there and shock the bewildered servants even more with lovemaking if necessary by force, he banged his plate on the table.

Julia went in the pony and trap again, thinking it was less conspicuous and the stable boy came again: he loved to take her, he was intrigued that she asked him and that she brought him a packed lunch with some extra for the pony. His name was Joe.

Julia knocked at the door and a smiling servant said yes Mr Potts was at home, would she like to wait while enquiries were made? In fact the whole house became curious about the well-dressed lady arriving alone leaving her pony and driver on the village green. This was one of those homely houses, a little untidy and informal with lots of books and children playing.

The first person to come into the room where she was waiting was Jack, the doctor's son. Julia got up rather staring at his handsome face and he gesticulated for her to sit down wondering if he should sit also and begin to blurt out things about Sarah and himself. Should he mention his love and grief for young Jack yet surely he was not meant to know that this was his real and bereaved Mother, the Mother lost to him at birth and so like him in looks.

The door opened again and a handsome but rather grave older man stood and looked from her to Jack and back. "Did you wish to see me, Madam?" Jack turned with a sharp look at his father and turned, pausing at the door, to ask Julia if she would like a drink such as coffee – she was rather pale. His startled father looked back at him and said, "Yes they would both have one." Mr Potts felt that his son knew more about this matter than made sense but it struck him with a little bit of alarm that surely this lady was Mistress to Sarah who they knew Jack had grown fond of, if not a lot more. Jack went off to order it with a quiet reassuring smile at Julia.

Julia felt rather overawed and wordless – Mr Potts was a rather grand and obviously famous high-placed surgeon, she was and had been a silly pregnant girl, what did she have to say to this gentleman?

Then she remembered the kindness of the parson and words began to flow.

"I think the boy, Jack who you looked after at the parsonage was my son. I had him when I was about fifteen." The great man had seated himself opposite her at the desk and now did not move or speak. "I went to the parson and Jack's grave." She paused as the tears came, "and now I'm pregnant again so this will be my fourth child and my husband is very angry since I told him about my first. He thought this would be my third child." The enormity and sadness of it were worse when she said it out loud.

Mr Potts was still silent; meanwhile the maid had brought him their coffee. The maid carefully pretended not to see the woman who she thought she recognised as the maid Sarah's mistress, the woman was weeping and turning away in her distress.

Mr Potts let Julia find something of control upon stirring his coffee. He and Julia had barely spoken before socially having been at the same gatherings infrequently. Mr Potts had spoken recently to the parson who had said he may have met young Jack's real mother; he and his wife had both recognised the lady from other occasions, both knowing Julia's friend Isobel.

Thinking quickly now Mr Potts realised he knew this lady's husband and that Julia's nursery maid was? Sarah who the Surgeon realised his eldest Jack probably loved; they had all grown closer while they cared for young Jack and he suspected that Jack and Sarah would now wish to marry despite being from such different social worlds.

Julia had the look of young Jack, the large eyes, the curls and polite manners and lovely profile. Mr Potts sat in silence because he knew Julia needed to get all her sad words and reminiscences out and because he felt himself conflicted by his own emotions, his own memories of sad young Jack and the lady's connection with his own Jack, through her maid.

"Your boy was a good lad," he heard himself say quietly. Even the parson had not been so direct and complimentary. The tears flowed even more. "Drink a little of that coffee," he suggested and turned a little away from her as she struggled for composure. To give her time he walked across to the window and looked out turning his back to her and shaking his head at his two youngest children who had noisily come to look in at the window – they loved to see their father at weekends – he was away a lot in the week.

"I should not have come," he heard her mumble.

"Yes, you should," he said in a quiet and kindly voice, "for your sake and mine, and for the parson and his wife, we will all keep this confidential but this will help all of us to try to get it in perspective," he paused. "I believe our own Jack will be part of this confidence we share, I think he may know already, he is a friend of your maid, Sarah, I think. They met while we all looked after Jack." He did not know that he had sighed, Julia was relieved to have a little change of subject- he was worrying that he'd said 'while' we were all looking after Jack to Jack's bereaved parent who didn't or couldn't look after him herself.

"I know this is difficult for you and your wife because she is a maid but she is a lovely girl and seems very fond of him. Not that I know..." She paused seeming to have said far too much.

"That is as it may be – she has had a sad and difficult life like so many of these young women," he did not say ladies – Julia was a lady by birth and she also had had a sad and difficult life he thought. "I thought I might try and help in getting the soot merchants to stop this practice." Her head went down again as she envisioned her son in a perilous and dirty climb.

"You ladies can be a great help to me and these boys by not employing soot merchants who use these poor boys," He wished he had not said poor, this lady was rich and well, her son had been thin, malnourished and pitiable. Mr Potts cleared his throat and then to clear his thoughts, this would not help this grieving woman who had sons now who were well and had a wealthy life. "I am not a sweep but I'm sure brushing works well and," he cleared his throat, "chimneys are starting to get smaller and more manageable again." He was rather relieved to have a new subject of discussion and chimneys and their ills was one of his favourites, he hated the effect this trade had on these young boys who usually had no one to protect them – as Jack had not had – until it was too late, as this sad mother realised.

Mr Potts had to hope that he could protect them in the future with legislation – for Julia and her family's sake. She was pregnant, he thought, as he'd been told she certainly did not need all this worry and when she had completed her family she could start to help the boys of this trade.

"Mr and Mrs Weaver looked after your son very well until the end... that Christmas" He realised he had said your son as a fresh set of sobs told him that she had heard those words too. He wished somehow that he could have prepared himself for this interview, it was difficult to put into words what had actually happened without giving this woman offence. She had not been there – she had not looked after Jack, her son. He studied his coffee cup then went quietly back to sit opposite her – thinking someone near may help her.

"I was able to help too, it will help you perhaps to know that both families made a fuss of him during those three months," 'his last three months' he stopped himself from saying – he still kept quietly talking thinking it would help her. "I think my Jack read to him and Sarah was like a sister in a way." Was this helping?

"There were two maids he was fond of." Yes, a description of events must help her. "One is a pretty one he was shy of because he liked her and an older one that he loved – Nancy, who was an excellent nurse to him and also sang to him a lot I think – bawdy songs I expect," he laughed a little, Julia tried to find a smile.

Mr Potts thought perhaps he had gone too far – he had said Jack had loved Nancy, and he had. Jack had not had one opportunity in his entire life to love this very sad woman, his real mother.

"The parson hired a man called James," yes they had had most of the expense in Jack's keep but Julia must know that. "He was very good with Jack." His words all seemed to be a sword in the mother's heart that others had met his needs and looked after him so well – but they had.

"He loved horses, your boy. Apparently he had loved the soot's cart horse," silly he should not have mentioned the man, the cause of the illness. "The parson had two in the field opposite the house…" He paused her head had gone down and her hands were up at her face but he continued. "We all went over to an early Christmas party – Jack loved all the candles and decorations. He loved firelight your boy." Should he have said your boy? He was sure she wanted him to describe these last days. More tears, more pain, she nodded for him to go on.

"I cannot pretend otherwise, your boy had had an extremely hard life – he probably was not well treated when he was a sweep. They did not realise how ill he actually was I must add, but I can say I watched the parson's family and the servants rally round in a wonderful way." He put his cup down and spoke more as a doctor. "Do not distress yourself more than this my dear – you know you have your own growing family, they are your priority now. I'm sure your family acted in what they thought were your best interests all those years ago."

He left her to go to the window again as she had slumped a little again; he thought he had been a bit harsh but he thought he had helped her face the reality of her life history that had been so separate from young Jacks. Of course he did not know that the marriage was at breaking point, nothing in Julia's life was going well it seemed to her.

Jack had already left the house riding over to Julia's house to openly ask if he could see Sarah in his unplanned but fervent haste. He was made welcome by an astonished maid who when he asked if he could see Sarah today, if not tomorrow – made them gasp as he was a gentleman and this was the front not the back of the big house. He had found that he wanted everything to be out in the open – it was as though young Jack in his tragic death had shown them how to be more real with each other. The maids left him in a side room and after whispering together they decided they must tell the Master who they knew was reading with young George upstairs.

The maid went up and nervously said to her Master but also with something of a gleam in her young eye, "There is a gentleman called Mr Jack Potts asking to see Sarah, the maid, sir, at the front door, what should we do?"

Sarah at this time was sadly tidying Julia's room she was very happy that she worked at this house but the atmosphere had been so depressing recently. Albert Sutcliffe stared at the maid in astonishment then got up and walked past her telling the maid to look after George and leave the rest to him, by which they the maids understood they were not to tell Sarah.

Albert went down to Jack and asked the young man to seat himself. They had met before socially but this meeting felt very awkward. They settled themselves and Albert rang for some refreshments to give the young man – partly to give himself a little more thinking time. He was somehow acutely aware that Jack had probably made love to Sarah already or he would not be here today, publicly asking for her. They must be betrothed or wanted to be. He felt sad and envious of all men who made love to women at this turn in his own life – it was difficult for him to sleep alone.

"Am I right in thinking you want to marry my wife's personal maid, Sarah?" Jack did not answer straight away using as an excuse for his silence that their drinks had arrived. Jack was unsure of what Albert knew – he was quite a lot older than Jack and had been married twice and had children and Jack had just left Albert's unhappy wife in a very upset state in his father's house.

He blurted out, "Your wife is at our house in the village seeing my father who is a doctor." Albert thought quietly was it about the presumed pregnancy, was something wrong? Or was it about that sad matter from the past? They were both silent, both in deep thought, trying to follow today's difficult events and wondering what each other knew of past events.

Thinking quickly Albert then said, "I think it would help if I drove you back in the carriage to your home with your horse tied up perhaps? Or you could ride it and we could take Sarah with us, she's good with my wife."

Was Albert proposing the right thing? Anything was better than the present confusion surely. He could not feel worse than during these recent weeks with the rift with his beloved wife. He got up decisively and rang for a maid to send Sarah down to them, and also had the carriage ordered without further explanation.

Sarah soon came looking very shy but unable to hide her delight in seeing Jack who simply went across to kiss her openly, even in front of the maid just about to go through the door and in front of Albert. "We are going to get your Mistress at my house." Sarah blushed and did not really follow what Jack had said in her acute embarrassment at being kissed in front of the severe-looking Master.

Soon the carriage was announced after a rather tense silence for the Master and urgent whispering between Sarah and Jack. The three quickly got out and into the carriage to drive the seven miles all sitting rather quietly deep in their own thoughts.

They arrived at the village, driving past the staring open-mouthed stable boy who was just then enjoying the lunch Julia had provided for him – he was sitting in the trap with the horse happily grazing. He grabbed at the reins seeing Sarah waving at him from inside the garage. The Master himself sat aloof not seeming to see much at all. The boy shook his head and after the carriage had turned the corner to the doctor's house he dropped the weight back down with a 'phew'. He loved his job, the master's house was thought to be the best in the area to work for but just lately it seemed a troubled unpredictable place.

The doctor heard a carriage arriving and went back to look out of the window and was mesmerised as he saw his son, Julia's husband and a very shy-looking Sarah, in a pretty maid's uniform get out. "Your husband is here with your maid, stay there," he motioned to Julia to sit back down. "I'll go and see him and offer him some refreshments, shall I?" This was his house and a servant had arrived in a carriage and this poor woman was uninvited he thought grimly but the doctor in him took over. "Let's do this as best we can – all of us," he muttered. He wondered what he would say to this maid. He left Julia alone in the room, shutting the door, his house door – very firmly behind him!

In the hall – he held up his hand to the three of them and with his natural authority asked his son and a very red in the face Sarah to wait in the room the other side of the front door – Sarah could not have curtseyed lower – and then took Julia's husband into another room and followed him with a Master's look back at the maids in the hall who were hovering in disbelief, staring at the door through which Sarah, a maid had just gone through to be alone with the Master's eldest and heir.

Doctor Potts became rather formal. "As your wife's doctor for the pregnancy should she need one – I would advise you to look after her and the sons she has already given you." Looking straight at Albert both had quickly sat down, "And if I were you I would try to let the past go if she has told you anything of that. Sometimes families are forced to find a solution for the best."

He paused, Albert just stared, rather red in the face as his private business was being discussed but calm. "She is here," continued the doctor, "as you know or I do not think you would be. She is extremely upset which is not ideal as she thinks she is pregnant." And then he said trying to be a little more kindly, "Shall I show you through to her?"

No assistance from servants was requested – he motioned Albert to quietly follow him through to a still very emotional Julia who in shock and surprise did not get up but just stared upon her husband.

Mr Potts quietly turned and left the room shutting yet another door with a purposeful click. He seemed to be having an unplanned morning of organising a lot of upset people to talk to each other, behind closed doors. He himself after shutting this last door stood for a moment trying to get a grip of all these events and then turned to the left to his study for five minutes and a drink.

Albert went swiftly to his wife kissing and hugging her tenderly. She fell against him in her loneliness and exhaustion and then led by his hand had followed him out to go home in their carriage. Albert even had the wit on this unpredictable day to get a bemused coachman to stop so that Albert could call out to the quickly standing stable boy "to get back home when he cared to". The boy Joe respected his Master and Mistress but "when you care to" are not usual instructions – so he just looked at the pony who looked back at him – Joe smiled and tickled the pony's ear.

"Right," he said leisurely still smiling, "We'd better get back when you're ready." The pony went back to grazing – no point in wasting time – so the boy sat on the grass in the sunshine – he hoped this job would last forever – before they were hitched up for the return journey the pony had even had Joe's lunch apple – Joe was too perplexed to eat it himself. And food for the servants was always plentiful at the house so it was not a problem losing his apple – so eventually when they cared to, boy and pony had a leisurely ride back with a lot of stealing and cropping of tasty leaves on the part of the pony and some tuneless bawdy songs from the boy – who felt like the king of the road.

In the fast-moving carriage in front, Albert just held his wife – kissing the tears away – to think they had a new baby to look forward to, perhaps a beautiful daughter? The tears and thus the comfort kept coming. Julia was utterly spent but gently kissed her husband back in her relief. They did not notice that the carriage had arrived back at their house in their relief to be holding each other again.

The coachman coughed, "S-Sir," Albert helped his wife out and up the steps waving everyone away and took her to her room, where he helped her off with her cloak and helped her to lie down and then as her head turned away a little to the wall he sat down on the seat near the bed thinking that in a minute he would leave her remembering what the doctor had advised but she quickly turned and made him get in with her.

Chapter 22

Jack and Sarah – Consequences

Jack had felt a mixture of emotions as his father shut the door firmly behind himself and Sarah. They both stood still for a moment – everything was happening so fast today. Jack knew that this was all rather his fault, he seemed to have sent this fast ball of events rolling. He looked at Sarah standing so still beside him as he held her hand, she was very red in the face and near to tears which worried him. He squeezed her hand, she squeezed back but left him to sit on the divan to their right – he followed they sort of flopped down together.

"The maids?" exclaimed Sarah, "Your maids," she clarified, gazing round at him. "Don't worry the house is rather upset today, Julia is here," he answered, they had not really spoken much in the carriage as the two horses had gambled on. Mr Sutcliffe had sat on one side looking out of the window, not at all at them and they had fallen silent. Sarah found herself pushed right into the centre of events, into the centre of Jack's life and perhaps the centre of the explanation of young Jack's death – she had had no preparation – she was naturally a private person.

It had almost been light relief when the coachman had slowed down the horses seeing his stable boy on the village green, who jumped up guiltily – he was still eating his lunch. The three servants were in deference to the Master thinking Albert might have new instructions but Albert just stared forward because Albert knew round the corner in front of them was Dr Potts house and his wife.

So the coachman just winked at Joe and told the horses to 'trot on' while Sarah gave him a small wave – Joe didn't have time and the nerve to wave back.

Then they were quickly up to the house and soon inside and there was Dr Potts to meet them. Sarah had great respect for the doctor for the way in which he had looked after her 'brother' Jack but she also had some fear of him, especially now as she was in love with and making love with his eldest son and heir. Immediately she was ushered into a room and was now sitting next to the heir, the maids had stared at her with frank astonishment with little enough time even for envy.

Jack went to the heart of the matter, "Julia is here – very upset – I think she was Jack's real mother years ago." Years ago, and that was the real difficulty something huge had happened to the baby and the young mother and somehow it now had something to do with all of them, they were all affected.

Jack and Sarah had gradually fallen in love as they had got used to losing the boy Jack, it was a mutual passion that they were joyful about but were also afraid of because of the strange circumstances of its inception – the sad death of a young man. Their life situation could not be more different – Sarah often stared down as she did now at her slightly work and cold-roughened hands. Julia was always giving her different creams, but Sarah knew for all the creams, that her hands were not those of a lady, not a lady of Dr Potts social class. And her voice, which was naturally quiet, did not have the assured vocabulary of Jack's siblings and friends, she knew that. Thanks to Julia again her dresses were now very pretty – they were in fact those of a lady and Sarah thought them inappropriate for her.

"I love you," said the man beside her.

"I love you too, but should I?" Her hair was now a little untidy under her pretty lace cap that Julia liked to see her in, a ladies maid cap!

Their nearness on the couch and the large emotion of such a momentous moment made them turn and gently kiss. "I should go to live somewhere else – you need a better, more suitable woman." She laid her capped head on his shoulder.

"I won't have another woman," he warned. "I'll marry you or not any."

She thought of recent times, Jack, the sweeps, Jack's death, the widow in her lovely cottage and then Julia and her growing family and her own reputation in the village and town and now Julia's reputation that few hopefully would know of; and then here she was beside the man she adored – quite well into her marriageable years at about twenty-two – they were about the same age these two lovers but, she thought quickly of the mirroring of lives and situations. Young Jack had been born to wealth but had died due to poverty. Her Jack born to privilege seemed to love her just a maid; born herself into poverty and work but rising up through the social class system, it seemed, entirely due to young Jack's illness and death.

Sarah had met her Jack because of young Jack's sad illness. Here she was in his father's house, the famous doctor, in his parlour. Would Dr Potts be coming in to see them? That is why they were here surely; he wanted to and would hear of their marriage plans – she was not sure that she had the nerve to sit here and face Jack's parents.

And she, like Julia, had made love; indeed wanted to know very badly – outside wedlock and for not the first time she thought of the real possibility of pregnancy. She was now forced to think of it – she had avoided thinking of it much before. If this family rejected her would she be alone like Elizabeth had been all those years ago with a child in an industrial town, where you had to work to survive. No other man would probably have her, she knew Julia would help her but knew that Julia worried she was making her same mistake, despite knowing what can happen.

And yet she knew she lived for the touch of Jack – she knew she would willingly follow him down to London and live as his mistress if he wanted her to. She had not dared to think of marriage, as a reality, even when he wanted to persuade her it was a possibility.

The door opened and Dr Potts came in.

Mr Potts did not realise or hear himself but he gave quite a big sigh as he came in and sat down on the other side of the room. A horrified Sarah had made to get up but Jack had stopped her then he did let her get up as his father sat down grimly. He had seen Jack had almost had to keep Sarah up and they stood together, Jack not smiling, holding her hand and Sarah very red now and trembling a little – her instinct was to run. Behind, but not heard by them, Albert and his wife were just quickly doing just that – getting away, wanting to get back to their home to try to deal with all this pain; and repair their marriage – if they could.

Had Julia known her maid was inside the house and having such difficulty even then she might have hesitated so as to help her because of her connection with both of the Jacks; Sarah and Julia had yet to really talk it all through and describe to each other all the separate events through those years that tied them together despite their different social standing, there was a deep friendship there.

Now Sarah was in the parlour and feeling rather alone, she knew that Jack loved her, but was she effectively Jack's mistress, with no real rights or expectations? Dr Potts senior was a famous and kind man and doctor and this his son was a younger version of his illustrious father, who at the moment Sarah was all too aware she was causing his lovely family a lot of trouble.

She felt herself falling backwards to sit down because she had to; Jack let her and then sat beside her, perched facing not her or his father as something like a bridge between two worlds.

Nobody had spoken yet then Dr Potts surprised them and indeed himself with what he said. "Mrs Sutcliffe was indeed young Jack's mother..." he paused, "I think she had Jack when she was about fifteen and the family thought it was best they separated them, mother and child..." he paused. Had he been involved in his doctor practice over the years in separating a mother and child? He did not think so, hoping he had not – but circumstances could be so difficult?

As he saw as he looked across at his eldest now determinedly soothing his love's arm with a gentle loving patting and he saw the girl who had always seemed so in awe of him now – looked rather petrified. Her hair had fallen loose and her eyes were downcast.

Dr Potts sighed again and sat back, then he got up and rang for a maid without thinking there was a maid already in the room. "I think we will all have a hot drink!"

The maid came in quickly with another behind her thinking things were very bad and help may be needed. The two had been eavesdropping at the door. Their loyalty at this moment was to a fellow maid but jealous feelings were there too.

"Things are all right now," explained Dr Potts without needing to, "let's have some tea." The normally friendly Jack did not look up at the maids and Sarah turned away a little, rather timidly.

"You two want to get married, I think." Dr Potts' words were coming out quicker than he could cope with – he put his hands behind his back clasping them as though he would stop up his mouth and thoughts to give himself time to think all this through. This was a second serious situation on this unforgettable Saturday morning.

He started to pace as in silence they all waited for the hot drinks to come – in a long and illustrious career he had seen so many tragedies – this morning he had seen the immediate effect of an inappropriate loving by a young girl and he wondered whether this girl was already inappropriately pregnant with his first grandchild?

Jack wore that determined look that he sometimes showed, when he first crossed swords with his father. They got on well but both were determined characters.

The tea arrived again with two maids – a third hovering at the door, they made quite a long procedure of it in their fascination, now moving in a small table conveniently near to Sarah, with her cup upon it, they were trying to catch her eye – with both loyalty and curiosity as a motive – would she be thrown out they wondered? Was she pregnant? They looked in horror and they knew the kitchen was spellbound waiting for news.

Sarah longed to drink the tea for she needed it, she was so immobilised by her fears, but then she did take a little drink – rattling the cup with her nerves – she was beginning to realise indeed that she might be pregnant, she did not feel herself and had been a little sick.

Jack moved to get his cup from next to her the maid had reluctantly quietly left – tiptoeing as though at a funeral. Sarah had only sipped her tea, now the pot came back in refreshed – before her was another cup and it occurred to her she really was taking refreshments with two gentlemen doctors in a social setting, she was afraid she would drop the cup. There was a long silence as they drank and considered...

Mr Potts had asked the maids as they left to find Mrs Potts who now came in with the curious two maids, the servant's informers, and with a cup for their mistress. Mrs Potts looked at her husband and then at Jack who looked back at her with a look of appeal, then she sat down.

"Julia was Jack's mother," she looked to check the door was closed, speaking confidentially – she was glad her husband had not called her into see Julia during their troubled tearful interview. But here they all were with this next trouble to deal with – young Jack had certainly made big differences in his short life.

She and Mrs Weaver had watched Jack and Sarah fall in love, knowing it was happening partly due to everyone's sorrow at the boy's young death bringing everyone closer.

Both mothers liked Sarah, as much as Julia herself did in fact, it was hard not to like her – her worth had been shown in her love of young Jack in the guise of a big sister. She was naturally polite and hard-working, an ideal maid in fact.

But she was a maid, and only a maid and Jack would one day probably be as famous as his father in the apothecary profession. Like the parson's family, the Potts were well aware of the social divisions and the ill effects of poverty, all three houses made sure their servants were well fed and as well rested as could be hoped for. They knew that sometimes it did happen that different social classes did intermarry. Her own thoughts and tea were interrupted by the unexpected. Sarah now got up, she realised she had not got up on Mrs Potts entrance, because the two gentlemen had not and she did not want to draw attention to herself in front of the maids. She felt absurd, which is why she acted now from sheer courage and she got up – Jack tried to get up too with her – but she stopped him, with a hand on his shoulder.

"Ma'am... I apologise for... I do love your son, and I did love Jack." She took a deep gulp, "but now I'm a woman," unconsciously she drew herself up straighter and her face was serious, "This has all been difficult – thank you Jack, NO!" as Jack tried to get up again – "I'm going to walk to the green and go back to my mistress with Joe... she'll need me today because of Jack's death."

Quietly she bowed to Mrs Potts and with a dignity she did not know she had she quietly left the room – confronting the three maids crouching outside with a quiet lift of her head and she went out the front door – having some difficulty with its heaviness and not able to shut it, she went down the steps and walked out to the lane and round the corner – with a lot of pairs of eyes seeing her go.

Joe and the pony were of course no longer on the green he had already set off. She hesitated there – seven miles? But then, she did not know word had spread next door to the parsonage via the servants and Mark and Ruth had been hovering and now approached and drew her towards their house, taking her round the back to the kitchens and soon Mary Weaver came through and took her into the parson in his study.

They sat her down and more hot drinks came – nobody said much – the Weavers guessed that Jack and Sarah were probably lovers by now – Julia's predicament from the past might be Sarah's predicament now?

As a parson, Mr Weaver knew more of these situations than the doctor: they had seen such consequences down the years. They were very fond of Sarah but it was not really their business apart from their wish to be her friend at this time. This was a matter only Jack and his parents could decide. If Sarah was not already pregnant and they hoped she was not for her sake, they did not think she had intentionally tried to trap a gentleman husband as some women probably think. The situation had occurred because a young man they had all grown fond of tragically died – a deep love had been born out of the situation. The Weavers both felt this was a very deep love.

Again...

Jack had felt a mixture of emotions as his father had shut the door firmly behind himself and Sarah. They both stood still for a moment, everything was happening so fast that day. Jack knew that this was rather his fault, he seemed to have set this rather fast ball of events rolling.

Chapter 23

Jack and His Parents

Jack did not follow Sarah as she had indicated for him not to. Instead he walked about the room and then went to the window – he could just see her disappearing around the corner into the lane. He knew that his mother was sympathetic about the situation but was worried and his father was probably very reluctant to let his firstborn and his heir marry a servant girl.

Jack sat down again and drank his tea, for something to do more than anything. He did not look at his parents but they looked at him.

What if she was pregnant? It would be a joy to him and their first grandchild.

"I want to marry Sarah and move her to London to set up in practice perhaps, and have a family." There he had said it, they did not speak.

Dr Potts was not a political man, had no interest in such power, an expert on medical matters – he did believe there should be more equality but also he was very much part of the establishment and the social order and had never envisaged his children marrying from the servant class.

Jack sat down – and his father went to drink his tea in front of the fire – he really wanted to go and talk to the parson but he looked across at his wife, who was looking just at her son.

Inevitably, he knew this would all be decided by himself probably – he could not stop his son from marrying anyone – he was of age, disinheriting if he did was at the moment unthinkable – that course of action could lead to family feuding and such tragedies as young Jack.

"We'll talk no more of all this today, Jack – we've all had enough for now, I don't want to worry your mother any further." The parents got up and Jack quickly went out of the room and Dr Potts told his wife, "I'm going to talk about all this tomorrow with the parson after church," he told his wife and she knew he would not have any more discussion of it that day.

"The parson knows Mrs Sutcliffe and Sarah better than we do," he patted his wife's wrist as he left her.

Jack's mother sat down again – she had seen the love between the two young people but they had all been so preoccupied with such a young death in their midst, emotions had been heightened for everyone.

***

And so, reader, Jack and Sarah were married the very next Saturday, everybody was there, Julia's whole household, the parson who married them and all their household, Dr Potts, as the groom's father and all the family – Jack's parents looking perhaps a little tense at the way things had turned out, but smiling because they thought their son would be happy.

Rose and her family were there. Perhaps a little envy played about Rose's lips but also she had invested some hope that Sarah's luck might help herself and her family. Surely, she had now climbed the social ladder a little after her sister? Rose's children would surely benefit?

And a lot of the village came – young Jack's old friends, some already courting now; there was an open invitation to the village with a reception on the green, from the parish.

The soots had gone. Rose did ask Jessie's new owner if she could pull the cart for the family, which delighted the bride; and the stable lad.

Joe came – Julia made sure he had a new outfit. The villagers commented later he had probably eaten the most – he would soon move down to London, to serve the newlyweds, with their horses.

Jack, the groom had only to walk past the parsonage to the church, with his brother on the day.

Sarah came with Julia and Albert in the carriage. Albert was to give her away.

Before however, when the carriage got to the church – the parson and his wife were there to greet the bride and before she went into the church they led her up a path strewn with petals towards young Jack's grave, which was especially garlanded with bright flowers so that in a way her young 'brother' was there as a witness at the wedding.

She was pregnant, their lovely baby girl was born at their new home in London – a girl – Sarah and Jack called their baby Julia.

And Jack the colt, now nearly grown, moved up to London with the young family and with Joe to look after him.

Three Jacks, one born to wealth, lost in poverty; the second well-born and married in love, with a good future before him. And a horse called Jack who, as a colt, helped an ill young man cope with the weakness and sadness of his last few weeks.